SERENA LONGHI GELATI

INSTRUCTIONS IN THE CAULDRON

Tradotto da Valentina Giglio

I.

The Holly Bush Cottage

It was Friday and like every Friday Sarah and I would go to our granny's.

The Holly Bush Cottage, as we called it in our family, was our second home, we had spent there every weekend and the summer holidays since we were babies.

A nice cottage in the English countryside, in Marlow precisely. Our great-grandparents had built it, our grandpa had inherited it later and it was inhabited by our granny Susan.

The house was composed of a living room, a kitchen and a dining room on the ground floor, three large bedrooms with two nice bathrooms on the first floor and a wooden attic with two large skylights opening on the surrounding countryside. I had spent so many evenings watching spellbound the clouds from up there!

Our pride was however the garden, where the big holly giving the name to the building dominated, followed by the oak near the gate and by a hawthorn bush, standing next to the main door. Of course, roses weren't missing, and lavender bushes, orchids, pot marigold and a small place dedicated to officinal herbs like sage, rosemary and mint.

Our parents ran a cafeteria called *Café Room* in Newbury, a nice wooden place whose specialities were, besides coffee, apple pies and *scones*.

Mum and dad didn't have much time to devote to us at the time. I wondered who would have looked after us if our granny hadn't been there. In my eight-years-old child mind, however, this problem was solved in a short time: granny was there and she would never go away.

I wished I could spend more time with my parents, the only time to stay with them was a week in Palma de Maiorca in the summer. I hated the cafeteria.

"You shouldn't talk like this, Anne!" my mother scolded me, "that is our job and it enables us to live a comfortable life".

I didn't exactly understand what "comfortable" meant, I only understood that my parents devoted more time to work than to us.

"Sarah, have you forgotten your rucksack at school again?" I reproached her when we got into the car.

"Oh, no, don't tell mum" she begged me.

"Don't tell me what?" mum asked, driving in the Friday afternoon traffic towards Marlow.

"I should have taken the M4 instead of going through Reading. Hell! It will take ages. I don't understand why your granny doesn't want to move closer and live in Newbury…it all would be easier".

The same old story every Friday, but our granny would never move, she would never leave *The Holly Bush Cottage* for anything in the world.

"By the way, mum, Sarah has forgotten her rucksack at school again!". I always felt a bit of fun in putting my sister under a bad light.

"Sarah! How will you be able to do your homework for Monday now?" our mum screamed, hooting at the same time to a big SUV which had cut her way. "People can't drive…especially on Friday evening. So Sarah, how are you going to do without your books?".

"I'll use Anne's books!" my sister answered innocently. She never got upset, even before the most resounding scolding, she just stared at you with her big eyes. Nothing could trouble her.

"Your sister won't be always there in your life. You must learn to be more responsible and to take more care of your things!". I didn't understand whether my mum was nervous for Sarah's fault, for the traffic or for the fact that the previous SUV was still before us and it was continually slowing down.

Even if it was almost dark, my granny was waiting for us in the garden, in her apron with pink flowers and a wonderful smell of apple pie associated with her.

"My two naughty little monkeys! Here are my girls!" she received us with a warm hug of the kind she was the only one who could give.

"Where's Sarah's rucksack? Forgotten again?".

"Yes, granny…".

"She would forget her head too if it wasn't attached to her neck! She's terrible, mum, terrible! Her teacher Richie is really worried, she looks as if she lived in a world on her own" my mother mumbled getting into the house with our bags in her hands.

"It's probably just like that, Rebecca. Tell me Sarah, what were you thinking about at school this morning?"-

"I was fancying I was already here with you, granny, sitting on the armchair in front of the fireplace, caressing Kiki…".

Kiki was my granny's big cat, black and lazy, he lived just for eating, sleeping and being fondled by my sister.

"I've been thinking about that all the while, but I've also listened a bit to the lesson, I swear".

"She has got a natural aptitude for visualization, my little witch!".

"Mum, please, don't tell her she's a witch! If she started fancying about that too, it would be the limit" our mother said in her usual brisk voice.

"I wouldn't consider it bad at all, Rebecca, really at all".

"And what about you, miss Anne? Always serious and composed?".

"One girl with her head in the clouds is enough, granny, isn't she?" I pointed out seriously.

I was the responsible and cynical one, sometimes even a bit nasty, but that was a part of my role.

Being a twin is difficult: you want to preserve your own identity, to make the world understand you're a single person and, to do it, you sometimes have to be completely different, not only in your clothes. I had asked my mother to stop dressing us up in the same way since I was five years old. I was tired that people always mistook us.

I would never want to change Sarah, I would be always there for

her, but my task was to show her the rational side of life, I didn't
have to nourish her fancies. I was just the opposite she needed to be
whole and she was the same for me.

"You must go now, Rebecca, or you'll be late!".

"If you lived closer, mum, it all would be really easier! There are
some nice little houses near Newbury…".

Mum was never going to stop insisting on making my granny move.
"Go, Rebecca, go…You know I'll never move! It's more likely
you're going to move closer in a few years' time…".

As soon as my granny received us at hers, it was as if we were
thrown into a different reality: the sweet smell of the apple pie just
taken out of the oven could be felt more intensely, the cat Kiki
arrived, scraping against Sarah's legs, the fireplace made the house
still more comfortable and our granny's love wrapped us like a
warm mantle.

We sat in the living room, on the old flowered sofa, we plunged
among the cushions and enjoyed telling her how we had spent the
week.

"There's a new girl in our class, she comes from London!" Sarah
commenced with enthusiasm.

"Wow, from the capital city…What a big change! What's her
name?".

"Alison" I answered ready.

"She has just her mother and she's a *hippie*!" Sarah went on. It was
always like that with us: we spoke alternating, one turn for me and
one for her.

Our granny burst out laughing: "How do you know she's a *hippie*,
Sarah?".

"She told me herself. She is sitting at the desk next to mine. But I
don't know what *hippie* means…do you know, granny?".

"Of course! Hippies are the children of the flowers".

"Children of the flowers?".

"They used to wear colorful clothes, they loved Nature and they
sang " Put flowers into your cannons! It's better to love each other
than wasting time and energy in useless wars". To cut it short, they

were just like that…What does Alison's mum do to be a *hippie*? Have you ever seen her?".

"She dresses up exactly as you are saying, she's very beautiful, always smiling, with long blonde hair and she wears a pendant with a glittering white stone".

"It's not glittering!" I interrupted her.

"Yes, it is. It looks like a white rainbow!".

"Rainbows aren't white" I pinpointed.

"It might be a white Labradorite". Granny got up from the armchair, she moved to the casket where she kept her stones and took one light stone out of it.

"Exactly, granny. That's it. Have you got it too?"

"I've got plenty…they keep me company and they help me", she said, keeping turning some of them between her fingers.

"How can they help you? They're just coloured stones!" I burst out defiantly.

"No, Anne, they aren't just coloured stones! They are much more and I'll let you know them, when you grow up a little more. If Alison's mum doesn't before me…".

"What are our plans for the weekend, granny?".

I already knew actually, it was March, the weather forecast said it would be sunny, so we were going to get the garden ready to receive spring.

Life at our *cottage* was marked by season changes: we carved pumpkins at Halloween, at Christmas it was a triumph of decorations, with evergreens, cakes and candles…it was absolutely our favourite time of the year! We usually spent most of the time at home around the fireplace in winter, towards March we got the garden ready, at Easter we decorated eggs and we spent the long summer days outside, barefooted; our granny picked up lavender, sage, rosemary and mint in order to dry them and we went back to school in September, but just after we had prepared some jam!

"We're going to the plant nursery, girls: we're getting new mould, some nice little plants and some seeds; then we're going back home and we're putting the garden in order. Mrs Bray is coming too".

"The lady who lives next door? Why?"

"You see, Anne, even if she lives just on the other side of the fence and she has got the same sunlight, the same shadow, the same rain and the same ground as I have, she can't make even a daisy grow in her garden. She's always hoping I will tell her my secrets!".

"So why don't you?", my sister asked her naively.

"Because I haven't got any. Flowers and plants are living beings, they stay with whoever they want to and they need to be fed, not only with water and manure…They need energy as well".

"Electric energy?"

"No, silly girl. The power of our mind. We must think about what we are doing when we plant them, to instil our trust, thankfulness and also our desires into them".

"Alison's mum has put a fairy house in her garden. She says they are going to help her to make plants grow".

"I wish I could know what kind of plants is Alison's mum growing…".

"I can ask her, if you wish".

"No Sarah, it doesn't matter, thanks".

"Have you seen them, granny?".

"What?".

"Fairies!" my sister exclaimed, as if that was something obvious.

"No, darling, I've never seen them".

"Because they don't exist!" I claimed lofty.

"Anne, not all we can't see doesn't exist. I've never seen the Great Wall of China, but I know it exists".

"Of course! They have taken photos of it, it's real. Nobody has ever taken photos of fairies instead", I replied, crossing my arms on my chest.

"Because they don't want to and they show themselves only to the people they choose", our granny explained.

"I don't believe it", I finished.

"So you're never going to see them…".

"I do believe in them instead, granny!", my sister said.

"I had no doubts about it", our granny burst out laughing.

"In fact I believe Mrs Bray should buy a nice house for them and put it in her garden, so they can help her grow plants and flowers".

"No, Sarah. Mrs Bray is not the kind of person who believes in fairies".

"So", I suggested, "she should just talk to them. I heard in a documentary that plants react very well if we talk to them".

"That's true, my darling. It's exactly like that".

I really couldn't believe plants could hear us, they didn't have any ears! But it was worth trying.

"Look how your little twins have grown up, Susan" , squealed Mrs Bray the day after. "You're lucky you can see your little- daughters every week. My son never brings mine here. By the way, you're their maternal grand-mother, you know, you are the favourite one…".

Our paternal grand-parents lived actually on the Balearic islands, in Palma; they had got tired of the English weather, so they had moved down there when they had retired. We saw them once a year: they gave us plenty of presents, but they didn't even know our teachers' or our friends' names and they sometimes still mistook our names.

"So, tell me, which of you is Sarah and which is Anne?".

We stared at Mrs Bray with our big light brown eyes, my sister and I were completely different and in an absolutely voluntary way. Sarah had long blonde hair, she was thin and angular. On the contrary I had shorter dark hair, like my dad's. Nobody ever mistook us.

At the plant nursery, Mrs Brady never left our granny even for a moment; she was her shadow, she kept asking stupid questions:

"How much water should I give the roses?", "Where is it better to place the chilli vase?", "How long will rocket take to sprout?", and so on, all the time.

Granny answered her kindly, giving her lots of advice.

"Oh, Susan dear, you really know everything! How can you?".

Our great-grandmother Maggy had taught her everything, not only about gardening, but also about cooking and knitting. Her works were famous all over Marlow, her best things were scarfs, pullovers and pot holders, all of them strictly purple, violet or pink.

"Knitting helps me relax. The colour which makes the mind calm down the most is really violet", she used to claim.

She completed her works with some drops of lavender essential oil, then she gave her creations to her friends as a present, or she took them to the *Charity shop* at the end of the street.

Lavender oil was never missing at home; it had helped me a lot when I was a small child and I couldn't get to sleep: I remember my granny used to put some drops on my temples and my chest, then she used to massage it, telling a nursery rhyme three times:

"With lavender oil and the moon in the sky, shall my little girl have a quiet sleep tonight". So I could sleep all night long.

"Granny, do you believe Mrs Bray's garden will be as beautiful as yours this year?", my sister asked, placing carefully some vases along the outside wall of the house.

"Oh Sarah, I hope it will, for her, since she spent a lot of money at the plant nursery. You know what I think: you should only take what you need. There's no use of having lots of kinds of flowers, if you can't deal with them or lots of different herbs if you don't use them and you don't know what to do with them. That's why I only keep the necessary ones; lavender, sage, mint, roses, pot marigold, hawthorn, laurel and rosemary are never missing. I also like geraniums, orchids and of course I couldn't do without the oak and the holly, but for them that's a different question…they keep me company when you aren't here".

Granny never had rest when we weren't there. There were always her friends coming and going to see her.

"They are always telling me their troubles", she had explained to us, "sometimes talking with someone is enough to feel better, to break the dikes of the dam we built to protect our ego. While they keep talking, I make a good tea, I knit, I think about what they are telling me and in the end I give them the little work I made. In that way, as if by magic, sadness disappears".

"How can you do that?" I asked curiously.

"I've told you, I just have to let them give vent to their feelings and always think about what I'm doing. While I keep knitting and they keep talking, I imagine them at peace, light-hearted, so I can charge my work with a positive energy, instilling these nice thoughts into it. It's not difficult, but I need to concentrate a lot, so I use the violet so much, it helps me stay more focused".

I didn't understand much, neither did Sarah.

"Granny, I've heard someone saying that oaks should never be cut down. Is it true?" I changed the subject.

"Absolutely! Just like an hawthorn branch should never be torn, except for *May Day*".

"But how can you do, if the oak gets ill?".

"When an oak gets ill, that's a bad sign…however a part of the trunk must be kept there. Roots are as important as the outer part".

"The cut down trunk can be turned into a nice little table".

"That's true, Sarah, an oak should never be completely eliminated, especially when it's inside a private garden! The family would crumble".

Sunday evening always came too fast. When we heard the noise of our dad's car on the gravel, we were caught by a mix of happiness in seeing our parents again and of melancholy. They usually took us to a nice *family pub* for dinner on our way home and it was nice to be with them, during those uncommon moments together, but we also

knew that we were leaving behind us the magic of the cottage and of our granny.
Luckily our week went by very fast between school and the various volley ball and dance clubs, we came home tired in the evening, mum gave us dinner, she spent some time with us and then we went to bed.

II.

Passages towards other realities...

The following weekend was mainly rainy and cold.
"That's not bad", our granny told us. She always saw the positive side in every situation.
"The new seeds need also rain and I have a lot of work to do. Old Mal invited me to take part in our *May Fayre* at Higginson Park, I'll have my own stall! I'm going to sell mainly knitting and some herbal oils I produce by myself".
Old Mal was a dear family friend.
"That's great, granny! Can we help you sell?", my sister exclaimed enthusiastically.
"Of course, Sarah".
"Alison's mother used to have a stall too, when they lived in London, in Camden Town", she went on in her dreamy way.
"That's really a very large market!", our granny claimed, brushing poor Kiki.
"They sold stones, amulets, incense…you know, those little sticks which are sweet-smelling if you light them. But she said it has become too commercial now and she doesn't like it anymore. What does commercial mean?"
"It means that most of the goods are alike, they aren't original, they just follow trends. London is a tourist city, people goes to Camden expecting they can find some particular goods. There are various trends: *punk, rock, gothic* and *hippie*, but, as she said, they have turned into a commercial style, to avoid disappointing expectations and to be sure they'll sell. Unfortunately, everywhere is like that… excepting *Chalice Well's* gardens and the *Tor,* of course".
Our granny's family came from there, she always took a dreamy mood when she was talking about her village. We had never been there, mum said it was a den for crazy people and granny always

14

scolded her because she didn't understand the magic of that place.

"Is old Mal your fiancé?", Sarah asked her impudently.

We had always suspected it, but we had never had the courage to ask her.

"Absolutely not! He's just a dear friend, we keep company to each other. We've known each other for ages".

Granny had told us again and again that she still missed our grandpa; he had died ten years before. A heart attack, he had passed away from morning to evening, without any notice. Our mum was just eighteen, she had never got over the shock.

We liked old Mal, as she called him. He was tall, with greying hair and a smile which always made you feel well, he could have been the perfect fiancé for granny. He was kind, smiling and he always took strawberry candies for us. He was fond of horses, he had two, *Smelly* e *Shelly*, and he was ready to saddle them and take us for a tour whenever we wanted to. I always insisted on not riding *Smelly*. He was famous in Marlow because he organized the yearly *May Fayre* with stalls, merry-go-rounds and gastronomic stands. If it wasn't for him, the fair might not be so nice; at least that was what granny kept saying.

"While you are knitting, can we watch *Harry Potter*?", I asked as I turned on the TV.

"That's ok. I'm really curious, everyone is talking about that young wizard".

"Great! Dad bought us the first boxed set, we could watch the first one today and the second one tomorrow…", I suggested.

"We'll see…you know, I don't like letting you stay before the TV set for too long".

We crouched down on the sofa for the whole length of the film, spellbound by the story. We knew it by heart, but there was some new detail to be discovered every time. It was absolutely our favourite movie. Granny never stopped knitting, she only got up to make tea. I couldn't understand if she was either following the story or thinking about something else.

"So, did you like it?", I asked as soon as the film ended; I was curious to know her point of view.

"If I liked it? It's great, girls! The author deserves all the success she is having. Absolutely gifted, a fancy worth of a great mind". Granny was really enthusiastic.

"And you still haven't watched the second one!".

"I especially liked a detail", she went on, "The idea of platform 9 and ¾: creating a passage to get into a different reality…neither the usual doors in tree trunks like in "Nightmare", nor the holes in the ground like in "Alice in Wonderland". Do you remember, little girls, when Alice is following the White Rabbit? She falls into a hole and, after a nice flight headlong, she finds herself before a door".

We had watched that cartoon hundreds of times.

"Another clever idea is the transformation of Professor McGranit into a cat…really nice. I liked it. But children, that's not magic, remember that. That's fancy. Waving a magic wand and saying a formula quickly isn't enough. Magic is something more: it starts from our work on ourselves to understand what we want to change and why. And above all, it doesn't hurt anybody. Never! It sends away, but doesn't hurt. Life, God, Mother Nature, Karma or what you call it will punish the ones who behave badly. Remember that: tit for tat."

"You also taught us: don't hurt, don't be afraid", I went on.

"Exactly."

Someone rang the door at that moment. Who could it be? Tea time had passed and it was raining hard outside.

Granny ran to open it.

"Oh, Mal! Come in, what's happening?"

"Pizza! Pizza for the most beautiful women in the county! Someone should feed you…"

"Old fox; come in, it's a pleasure to have you here." She immediately took his umbrella and laid the pizzas on the table.

"Where are the two little monkeys? Here they are, they are getting more and more beautiful! Miss Sarah, Miss Anne, how are you?"

After a long bow, he took two strawberry candies out of his sleeve. I can't remember seeing him without them, even once. "The sweets

after the pizzas, girls. Now wash your hands and lay the table."
"You're so demanding with them, Susan."
"Rules, Mal. Rules."
"Yes, Madam! I see that the production for the stall has taken off: there's violet wool everywhere. Don't overdo it, Susan.
Mal was looking around himself bewildered: when our granny did something, she always put her best care in it. "I don't want to cut a poor figure, it' a honour for me to join it. Who is going to get the proceeds this year?", she asked him, handing him the glasses and the cutlery to lay the table.
"The proceeds will be partly used to build a town gym and partly for research on multiple sclerosis."
"Excellent Mal, as usual."
We spent a pleasant evening, between pizza with cheese and frankfurter, a Scrubble match and the old man's jokes. He didn't go away late, however we were already exhausted.

"Granny…"
"Yes Anne, tell me."
I was in my bed, but before she turned off the light, I had to tell her something: "When I come here, it seems to me I'm getting into another reality."
"What do you mean, my child?", she asked me, sitting down at the foot of the bed.
"Here at yours, I feel like Harry, when he goes through the wall at King's Cross Station."
It was something difficult to admit for me, my part involved not believing in those things.
"It might be like that…maybe it' s the old oak out there, next to the gate…"
My granny was smiling satisfied. Her big green eyes were shining and the light of the *abat-jour* made her red hair still brighter. She looked incredibly like Molly Weasley, Ron's mum in *"Harry Potter"*.

"Why the oak?" I didn't understand what the oak had to do with it.
"You should know that oak is *Duir* in Gaelic, which is where *door* comes from. And what's a door? An opening between two worlds, a passage. The ancient oak can open a passage for you, towards something nice. I'm happy, Anne, that you've told me. You are two special kids and I have the duty of teaching and passing all my knowledge to you, as time passes by."
She leaned and kissed me on my forehead.
"Will you teach us to make the best chocolate cake in England?"
"Not just that Sarah, not just that. Now you just have to enjoy your age. Childhood is a special time, you must play and stir your fancy. Good night my little girls, shall the Goddess bless you now and forever.".
Granny always talked like that before we fell asleep, I've sometimes heard my mum saying it too. I knew other children told Mary or Jesus their prayers, Alison and her mother lit a candle before Buddah's statuette, Aysha's family celebrated Ramadan instead…
Granny kept saying: "The important thing is to feel at ease with a deity, we can call and fancy it just as we wish to." She called it Goddess Mother, or sometimes Brigid or Ecate…I had sometimes heard her name also a Pan, which was in my mind Peter Pan.

III.

Days, colours and the wheel of the year

Three years went by. We were finishing primary school and we were already eleven years old.

Sarah had discovered pink nail polish, I, instead, hid myself into large black hoodies whenever I could. I had insisted upon having a school uniform one size larger than mine.

In these years we have witnessed Alison's mum's illness close, she fought hard against breast cancer; it seems she managed at last.

Sarah was shocked when she saw her without hair for the first time, she cried all night long. Mum explained to her that some treatments were really strong, but absolutely necessary.

"That's not fair, her hair were so beautiful!", she said between sobs.

"I know, darling, but they will grow again, don't worry", she comforted her.

"We should pass our positive energy to her", granny claimed when we told her what was happening. "Following the doctors' instructions is right, but she needs something more."

It was a cold Saturday afternoon at the end of October, the autumn colours in the garden were wonderful. The fireplace was lit and I could already breathe the typical *Halloween* atmosphere.

"I wish to explain something to you, girls", our granny began while she was putting into the oven her traditional apple cake, "I'm going to talk to you about the power of colourful candles and of the days of the week. It's really simple. We are going to lit some candles for Stella, she needs them." That's how Alison's mother was called.

"She always keeps some stones next to herself...", I added, thinking that was a fundamental detail in order to understand a person better.

"I'm going to explain that as well, one thing at a time, Anne! You called them colourful stones some years ago and I promised I would talk about their powers; you know I always keep my promises! All in due time."

"I still believe they are just colourful stones! And it looks absurd to me that some candles lit on certain days could help someone ill. Days are all alike!", I burst out as usual.

"That's not true…let's say that most of the energy, if not all of it, is strictly connected to moon cycles: waxing Moon and waning Moon. During the waxing phase, we have a growth: our nails and hair grow faster, we have a tendency to put on weight or to swell, so we should work on a growth energy; on the contrary, the wining phase moves away. You know, Anne, in the past people lived in close touch with Nature, they respected it and learnt from it. Every time in a month or in a years has got a different energy, we should understand when we can take advantage of it. Colours send powerful spurs to our brain", granny went on, "I've always told you that violet helps me relax and concentrate. Colour therapy is a serious science…" Not all the things she said appeared clear to me, she sometimes spoke about things I couldn't understand, but I would keep everything she taught me as a treasure, as time passed by.

"In this particular situation", she went on, "I want to help Stella to increase her physical strength and to detoxify from the remedies she had to take, poor woman. So I'll have to work both on a growth energy and on a moving away one; I'll try hard during the whole twenty-eight-days moon cycle. Have you understood, girls?"

"I have, granny", Sarah nodded. She liked listening to those things, they had always charmed her.

"Go on…", from my personal view, I felt attracted and reluctant at the same time. The influence of the Moon on human life was undisputed.

"Why are you doing it, granny? You don't even know her", my sister said while she was making Kiki play with a small ball.

"It doesn't matter if I don't know that woman, Sarah, I know she's feeling bad and I want to help her with the tools I have at my disposal."

"But she hasn't asked you for help."

"Good remark, Anne! By the way, don't you think it's evident that she wants to live, since she underwent an operation and such invading treatments, like chemotherapy? What's more, you told me she's keeping some stones next to herself, so she believes in the same energy as I do. She doesn't need to ask for my help, I know in the bottom of my heart that's the right thing to do." My granny's argument wasn't wrong. "Let's go back to ourselves, girls, make yourselves comfortable and take some paper and a pen, if you like."

She sat down on an armchair and Kiki climbed on her legs, purring.

"Oh granny, I've been looking forward to this moment for so long. Look what a nice notebook I've kept just for this occasion. I'm going to write everything you'll teach us", my sister got excited.

I couldn't believe it, my sister had just taken out a pink and glittered notebook.

"Sarah, you're ridiculous. How old are you, five?"

"Anne, stop making fun of her, I think it's wonderful."

"Yes, it's wonderful for a girl on her first year at primary school!"

"I'm going to keep here my notes about magic", Sarah exclaimed satisfied.

"We aren't at the pink Witches' congregation. You're ridiculous… that's enough, I'll leave!"

I got up and I ran upstairs. They were both completely crazy: the one with her ideas about energy, stones and candles; the other who was playing the fairy. I could understand by now why my mum had left home when she was just twenty! I preferred staying alone and listening to music.

After a while, however, I was lurking on the stairs. I didn't care about what they were saying, I just wanted to understand if granny would tell Sarah any important secret.

"I'm sorry for Anne, granny, she is always so nervous lately", I heard her say.

"Don't worry, my dear, it's normal to feel like that at her age. I'll make a good St. John's Wort tea for her tonight and you'll see she will calm down; your mother was just like her when she was eleven…she's still like that in fact."

Our grandmother never got upset, my sister had certainly taken after her.

"Granny…"

"Yes?"

"Can you tell about the candles just to me, or Anne needs to be here too?"

"Oh, of course my dear! If she doesn't care at the moment, I can't see a reason to prevent you from learning. Well, well…where am I going to star from?"

"From Monday?"

"That's right, from **Monday**: the day of the Moon, associated with **white;** it's the time to tidy the house, the garden and to make our intuition grow." She was talking slowly, to give Sarah time to write.

"Then we have **Tuesday**: Mars's day, the colour is **red**, it's perfect to solve tangled situations and to overcome clashes. **Wednesday:** it's Mercury's day, associated with **yellow**; on this day you can work on communication, on writing, on reading, to get a deeper inspiration and better possibilities of success, it's the perfect day to instil enthusiasm. Ah, **Thursday**, my favourite! It's linked to Jupiter, the colours are **green** and **light blue**, it's devoted to finances, fortune, plenty and wealth. **Friday** is Venus's day, the colours are **pink** and **green;** on Friday you can try to improve the sentimental sphere, love, friendship, but also beauty and body care. Try to have a *manicure* on this day, and you'll see how nice, healthy and strong your nails will get. **Saturday**: Saturn's day, the colour is **black,** excellent to move away and exorcize negative forces or to increase our wisdom. And finally **Sunday**: the day of the Sun, the colour is

orange, it's the day of the family, of *BBQs* with friends, lightness and will get stronger. After that, according to the colours I have listed, we can light a colourful candle on corresponding days. If we don't have colourful candles, we can use the white ones, they're always good for that! Candles are the symbols of thought, idea, desire and hope. The four elements are contained into them: the Earth is the wax; the Water is the melted wax; the Fire is the flame and the Air is the smoke. I've recently discovered floating candles: you put some water into a bowl, with some grains of kitchen salt to represent the Earth element, you put a candle on it and you light it. They are very beautiful and safe. It's always a good rule to oil the candle before you light it; you can use an essential oil from our production to do that, I'll show you how to make them, it's not difficult. Of course, you need to concentrate when you oil and light it, to instil our will to the candle. Now tell me: on which days can we help Sheila and which candles shall we use in your opinion?"

"To give her strength, a waxing Moon Tuesday, because you said that during this phase energy gets stronger, the colour of the candle will be red. To move away bad cells and the remains of remedies, a waning Moon Saturday instead, the colour will be black."

"Excellent Sarah, really excellent!", our granny clapped her hands satisfied.

"I'll add two very important colours: **magenta** and **purple red**. The first one works on our psyche fast, because it has the ability of awakening the magical power of our mind. The second one instead, is the symbol of Wisdom and it is used to move bad luck away. It's enough for today, Sarah, let's go and find your sister now."

I sprang up and went back into my bedroom without being noticed.

"Ok. Granny, do you really think we'll be able to help Stella?"

"You see my child, I could never replace traditional medicine; treatments are important, but doctors and science have left behind some other sides in time. There's always a reason behind an illness. The power of positive thoughts helps us to feel better; some people

go to church, they say the rosary, they go on pilgrimage or something like that, they firmly believe in what they are doing. You can't realize the power of our mind at all and the consequences of our words. You'll see, your friend's mum will get better, you mustn't stop believing it."
"Thanks granny. Let's go to Anne now, if I know her well, she must be starving.

Old Mal came to the *cottage* the next morning.
"Here you are, the best pumpkins in all Marlow, directly from *Sainsbury's*. Our girls are too grown up to play "treat or trick" along the road, but carving pumpkins is compulsory at all ages. We have to keep away the bad souls going around on that night…and don't forget to leave some gifts for them! Talking about gifts, I almost forgot, I've got just two strawberry candies for you."
He was always cheerful, he conveyed happiness just being close to him.
"Thanks Mal, you're always spoiling us."
"You are my favourite girls, it's normal I want to spoil you. Susan, I don't have any candies for you, but an invitation. You are going to be my "plus one" at Christmas dinner, to christen the new town gym."
"Oh, Mal…I'm left wordless! Thanks, I haven't gone out for dinner for ages. I don't even know if I have suitable clothes", our granny admitted pretending to be shy.
"Mum will lend you something!", I suggested.
Our granny out for dinner with Mal, that was really something new!
"Yes, Rebecca will lend you something. You are going to be very beautiful as usual. And then, the rebuilding of the gym was made thanks to you too, with all the violet potholders you sold at the last *May Fayre*. It took three years to raise the money we needed, but we managed at last, and what event could be better than Christmas to inaugurate it? The dinner will be on 21st December, isn't that great?"
"For Yule, that's wonderful! I hope there will be also a nice

decorated log."

My grandmother had taught us since we were very young the importance of seasons, equinoxes, solstices and of certain days such as *Halloween* or *May Day.*

Halloween was for her **Samhain**, the Celtic New Year's Eve; it stood for the end of the period of light and the entrance into the darkness of winter. Nature seems to die, it withdraws into itself, animals go into hibernation and also men withdraw into the warmth of their houses. It's a magic moment, when the curtain between the world of the living and the one of the dead gets thinner; for that reason it's a good habit to honour our dear dead, leaving gifts for them and lighting candles to help them find the light.

Our granny also explained to us that the pumpkins left outside are used to scare the damned souls who can't find their peace and want to annoy the living.

Wearing fancy dresses and going around asking for some sweets is just a parody of these dead souls, who ask for gifts and threaten to play bad tricks. I remember that, every time we emptied a pumpkin, she kept three seeds and put them into her purse.

"So money will never miss", she said.

Mal and granny called Christmas **Yule** and they celebrated it on 21st December, the day of the winter solstice, the period when days are really short and the cold is biting. She told us that solstice meant literally " Still- Sun".

"Do you remember, girls, when you get on the panoramic wheel and it stops at the highest point, and then at the lowest? Well, the Sun does the same thing. In winter the Sun is in the lower part of the wheel, it's more hidden, but it's there. During the solstice it stops for a while and then it starts to rise again. Christmas stands for the rebirth of the Child Sun, exactly like Jesus who was born in the darkness of a cave."

From that moment, days get longer again slowly; every year the same magic takes place with exactness. We decorated the house together with our granny with evergreens, which represented life going on, we lit candles, we put some mistletoe here and there, and it was compulsory to kiss each other under it.

The wooden log taken from our oak couldn't be missing in our fireplace, it was kept lighted during the whole period of the Christmas holidays, then granny gathered the ashes and spread them around the house, keeping telling: "May negative powers keep away from here!"

I couldn't understand very well what she meant by negative powers, I thought she was referring to unpleasant people.

When February started, the snow fell heavily and the wind blew freezing from the north, Mal punctually arrived at the cottage, with a new broom.

"A present for the wisest woman in the whole county", he claimed smiling and granny thanked him with a strange word. "Happy **Imbolc** to you!"

Granny told us that Nature was slowly waking up in that period, so we had to clean and purify the house. It was quite impossible for me to think already about spring, but I always started to notice some changes after a heavy snowfall or a winter illness: days were beginning to get clearly longer and some shy snowdrop was peeping out in the fields.

"Children, you must always remember that it's sometimes good to have fever, fire burns and purify. Shall Goddess Brigid protect and bless you."

We knew how much our granny was devoted to Brigid, she often tried to justify herself by laughing and saying: "Maybe that's because she has got red hair like mine!"

Everyone took her for an Irish woman. I think she had never been to Ireland; but to make up for it she always went to the Irish *pub* with Mal on St. Patrick's day. She didn't like particularly Saint Patrick, I was sure about that, she used to say that every year, but she could never refuse a beer in good company.

Soon after, **Ostara** finally arrived, on 21st March, the spring equinox: it was a period of perfect balance, with the same hours of light and of darkness. Nature had awakened at last! We used to spend those days painting eggs, which were a symbol of rebirth, and we got the garden ready going to the plant nursery.

Our new family tradition was taking with us our neighbour, who had shown signs of great improvements in the care of her plants in the previous three years.

"That's surely thanks to the gardener she has hired", our granny had claimed naughtily.

May was my favourite month: there was our birthday, Marlow's fair and Nature was at its best, with all those flowers blossoming, a delicious smell of jasmine in the air and the Sun warming us at last. Celebrations started with **May Day**, the first day of the month, which was also called **Beltane.** For that celebration granny used to give us some delicious flower wreaths she made herself and we hang coloured ribbons to our oak.

The 1st May was the only day when we could pick flowers from the hawthorn and we later left some presents for the fairies, like little crumbs or a bit of milk, because people said that those tiny beings were the guardians of the tree and so it was right to thank them somehow.

Granny asked Mal to add a big bonfire to the village fair, just like people used to do in the past at Beltane.

"That's quite dangerous, Susan, but we'll see what we can do…"

As foreseen, authorities never let them light a bonfire, but they replaced it with wonderful fireworks and with a tall pole around which people could dance braiding ribbons; they told us that was a very old tradition as well.

"It's not exactly the same", granny had said, "but it'll be alright too. What's more, children love that!"

Towards the end of school, when we were tired at last and it was hot in England too, it was **Litha's** time, the summer solstice, the longest day of the year! The Sun never set.

"You see, the Sun is high on the panoramic wheel, but it's going to start its descend slowly by now. Isn't that incredible, girls? That's all so perfect."

We put granny's stones outside at night and we spread a cloth on the grass; we took it back the next morning, before the Sun rose completely, soaking with dew.

"That's my beauty secret!", granny told us laughing and putting some drops on her face. "The summer solstice dew. You can't imagine what is this night's power!"

It was simply dew for me, but I must admit that I was particularly happy in those days when summer began and that was a real magic for someone grumpy like me.

As soon as we finished school, at the end of July, we left for Palma de Maiorca. The Baleares' heat and sun was really something strange for us. We spent whole days into at the swimming pool during that period.

"Rebecca, bring the girls to the seaside on 31st July at least, it's **Lughnasadh!** I'm not asking you to make bread with them at dawn as I do, but let them stay in the sun as long as possible at least. That's good. With a cap and sun cream, of course. Remember that, I'll warn you! I can't understand why you're always at the swimming pool, isn't the sea beautiful there?"

"Oh, yes mum, the sea is wonderful, but the swimming pool is more comfortable. With no sand, a café nearby and sun beds to relax…", our mum answered in a persuading voice.

"I don't understand…what's the use of spending the days on the edge of a swimming pool?"

"We go there to have rest, mum, we really need that!", she put an end to the conversation that way.

And then autumn came, Nature changed its colours, the garden at the cottage lost its leaves day by day, days get shorter and cold came back. **Mabon**, that's how granny called the autumn equinox. She decorated the table with ivy and she put into some pots the herbs she had been drying in the hot months.

"What do you need all these herbs for, granny?", Sarah asked her once, passing her hand through the well tied lavender, hanging by its long stalks.

"I can do lots of things with them: my oils, my tinctures, good luck little bags, and I keep them for my herbal teas. You shouldn't throw away anything, remember that!"

"How is that possible? You taught us that, before spring comes, it's important to clean the house: to throw away what is useless for us and give our old clothes to the poor!", I underlined obstinately.

"That's right, Anne. We mustn't accumulate, otherwise our house will not breathe and energy gets too heavy that way. Throwing away the unnecessary, that's right, it's foolish to keep too many things. I'm telling you not to waste: if I picked up so many lavender flowers, for instance, never too many or more than necessary, I'll use them all, I'm not going to throw anything away."

"When are you going to teach us to make oils and tinctures, granny?"

"Give things time, Sarah…"

"Why can't mum do anything you do? Why didn't you pass on your knowledge to her?", I asked her.

"You see, your mother is a woman who can be called hasty; she wants everything and at once. She was born in fifteen minutes, she got married and she was pregnant with you when she was twenty! Whenever she needs an essential oil, she goes to *Holland & Barrett* and she buys it, if she needs basil she goes to *Tesco* and gets it. She can't wait for the plant to grow, to pick it up, dry it and then wait as long as it is needed to macerate and give an herbal oil. I'm her mother, I know my Rebecca! I would have wasted my time showing all these things to her. But I really think she can do that all, since she saw me do it."

I wasn't as sure as her about that.

I wished I could know what she thought about me, if she really believed I would be able to work with herbs and stones. Maybe in the bottom of her heart she had already understood she could hand on her knowledge just to Sarah. I preferred on my part to avoid certain subjects, fearing I wouldn't match up, I preferred hiding myself and not believing in those things.

IV.

Christmas with Major Arcana

It was a cold Wednesday at the end of November, we were going to the volley club after school, as usual. We didn't expect to meet our parents when we went out.

"What are you doing here?", we asked them at the same time.

"Has anything happened?"

"No volleyball tonight girls, we are going home, dad and I have to talk to you."

That was something absolutely new. It could just mean something bad, but they looked relaxed and smiling instead.

"Are our grandparents well?"

"Of course, Sarah. Who's better than them?!", our dad stated. "All day long in the sun and on the edge of the swimming pool.

There are still twenty degrees down there in November, can you fancy that? That's wonderful."

"And what about granny?", I asked agitated.

"She is ok as well, my dear, don't worry. Nothing serious has happened."

"So why did you come and see us to talk?"

"Let's go home now, Anne, we'll have a good tea all together and then we'll tell you the news."

"Are you pregnant?"

"No, Sarah, I'm not pregnant. You two are enough for me!"

Mum might have been pregnant actually, there would have been nothing wrong, but she had always been emphatic about the fact that her supply of energy and patience had come to an end after two twins.

When we got home and we were sitting all together around the table, as we had hardly ever done, we discovered what the news was: we were going to move to Sonning Common.

"Where the hell is Sonning Common? And above all, why are we moving there? We're at our last year at school. How can you think of taking us away?", I burst out. I flew into a rage, I didn't want to go anywhere. I liked Newbury, we were born there and we had all our school mates there. Moving away was something absurd!

"Sonning Common is north of Reading, near Henley-on-Thames, we'll be just thirty minutes far from your granny's house!"

"Yes, but why? We're so well here in Newbury", I went on astounded.

"Your mother and I are going to open a *bio-veg* café. It's a great opportunity. Don't worry about school, you are ending the year here and you' re starting college there."

"So everything is already fixed…"

"Yes, Anne, everything is fixed. Mum has got two more good news to give you."

"Ok, fire away…it can't be worse than that!"

"The good news is I spoke with Stella about our move, you see, I didn't know how to face up to the question with you, so I asked her for advice too…Well, you see, she decided they are coming too! Isn't that wonderful? She is still under medical supervision and she needs to be looked after at a good hospital, the one in Reading is surely one of the best in the whole Berkshire. What's more, it's just twenty minutes far from London by train and her parents live there…So, we're going there all together. Are you excited, girls?"

The fact that Alison was coming too, was surely the best side of the situation. The three of us had been always very close; she was able to counterbalance my relationship with Sarah: she was balanced, methodical but at the same time sweet and sensitive.

Even if she had grown up according to *hippie/new age* ideals, she looked absolutely ordinary.

However, I wasn't quite persuaded about moving house.

"And what is the other news, mum?"

"They're coming to spend Christmas Eve with us at granny's! Stella wants to meet her. Don't you think that's a great idea?"

"Luckily old Mal will be there, otherwise I would be the only man among wonderful, but absolutely crazy, women", our dad claimed.

He wasn't wrong at all, actually.

That was certainly one of the funniest Christmas in our life.

In the afternoon we helped Granny to make *Christmas pudding*, stirring and making wishes, according to our family's tradition, while she told me how much fun she had had with Mal at the gym opening. She had even danced latin-american music and played bingo till midnight. Mum had laid the table with traditional red and golden colours, putting creakers on every dish. Dad and Mal were instead trying to make the fire brighter in the fireplace, using Yule's log.

At exactly 6 pm Alison and Stella arrived with a Christmas poinsettia and a bottle of *rosé*.

"I'm very pleased to meet you, Susan. I've heard so much about you", Stella told her with a hug.

"The pleasure is mine, dear."

"Sarah has told Alison about the candles…I was really moved, thanks a lot! You're a *wiccan*, aren't you?"

She had the bad habit of making people lots of questions. Alison said her mother had no philtre between her mouth and her brain. She was pleasant, always smiling and what's more she could listen to people, just like granny.

"No, darling, I'm not. I know the *Wicca* religion very well, I've spent my first years in Glastonbury…"

"That's where your strange accent comes from! That's great. But can I ask you, why do you live here now?"

"My husband inherited this *cottage* and I agreed to leave the "Apples island", I haven't been there for so many years…"

"This house has got a certain energy in fact, it looks as if we are in a different reality…" Stella was looking around herself, like little girls before dolls houses.

"That's strange, Anne said the same things some years ago!"

"I've been to Glastonbury too, soon after they had diagnosed my breast cancer…I needed to rediscover myself. A spent a whole afternoon sitting at *Chalice Well*, I stared at the well, the *Tor,* the water flowing: I was shuttered. I would never have expected such a difficult trial in my life. I do yoga, I'm master *Reiki* and crystal-therapist, I followed meditation courses in India when I was younger…I blame London air, it's so polluted. I don't know…Oh, I'm sorry, I'm talking freely about my problems…That's because you make me feel really at ease, Susan."

"I'm really pleased about that and you don't have to apologize at all", my granny comforted her. "You must be happy you're here now. Everything has come to an end; enjoy every moment of your life with your wonderful daughter and with your friends' fondness. Don't blame London air, that's true, it's polluted, but unfortunately some illnesses happen also if you live on top of a mountain! One of my cousins was vegetarian, she didn't smoke, she walked a lot and she lived in the South, near the sea; she fell ill all the same."

"I've learnt a lot from this experience", Stella went on. "It made me understand how frail we are. My stay in hospital was terrible! I hate places like that, the heavy energy, the deep pain, you lose your sense of time. At the start I didn't want to undergo chemotherapy, I didn't want to poison my body. I did all that for Alison. Keeping my mind focused on my target was so difficult."

"But you managed at last. Your holistic training has surely helped you a lot!", granny had always had this power, she could encourage people and help them see the positive side in everything.

"Yes, I'm sure of that. I devoted my time to the study of Tarots in hospital and during my period of convalescence, when I could read. One night I dreamt I was holding in my hands a small tin box with cards inside: they were "Maria Celia's" tarots, those cards really exist!". She took out of her huge bag a small tin box with cards inside. "I bought them online together with a book and I started this new course. I think you can read them…"

"I'm sorry to deceive you once more, but no, I don't know any kind of divination. I'm just used to consulting an oracle when the seasons change. If you wish, you could explain us the meaning of Arcana after dinner. I haven't heard about them for ages. My aunt Ruby, my mother's sister, could read them; she made a lot of money with them, she was famous in Glastonbury. Unfortunately, I haven't inherited her gift."

"Oh, I don't want to bore you."

"Just relax, the ones who don't want to listen to are free to leave the room. Let's have dinner now. Children, wash your hands! It's ready."

The dinner was delicious, granny was a perfect cook. She made traditional dishes: turkey filled with blueberries sauce and *pigs in blankets* (which were absolutely my favourite). Of course, vegetarian dishes for Stella weren't missing. Besides our *pudding* as a dessert, Mal brought a wonderful *Yule log*.

According to tradition, when dinner ended we exchanged presents. Sarah got a "Griffindor" hoodie and I got a "Ravencrow" one. After we had cleared the table, mum, dad and Mal started playing Scrubble, Alison and I sat on the sofa watching TV, with lazy Kiki next to us, while Sarah and granny were listening to Stella explaining Tarots.

She mixed the cards making her bracelets tinkle, she had a mysterious look, she moved them with skill and precision, as if they were an extension of her fingers.

"These cards can help us to understand the Divine project", I heard her say. "They don't foretell the future with certainty, but they tell us what could happen. It's up to us to understand them and to live what life gives us as a continuous teaching somehow. Cards are a means of divination, they keep us in touch with the real source of All and they must be handled respectfully. Let's start from Major Arcana, they are twenty-two. The first card is **The Madman-0:** it represents the start of a new journey. We sometimes throw ourselves into an adventure without thinking about it before, led by too much enthusiasm. Being able to take a risk using our hidden gifts is very important."

She turned to Sarah and my granny that small card representing a young man on journey with a stick, held back by a little dog.

"Then we have **The Magician-I**: the wizard, the one who focuses on something and turns it into reality. He knows he is the means the Divine Spirit appears through. We are the makers of our fortunes, just like the man in the card who works with his tools to get what he wants and to evolve.

We then find **The High Priestess-II**: she is the symbol of intuition and wisdom. We must be able to keep detached from the material world and listen to the voice of our guide spirits; only by knowing ourselves we will be able to understand the world surrounding us. Can you see the eyes of the woman in the drawing, lost in her thoughts and far away? It looks as if she could see beyond everything. I think she reminds me of an oak, strong and still.

The Empress- III: this card brings romanticism, love and sensuality. It's the symbol of a happy moment, full of creativity and emotional fertility. She could be compared to spring, to rebirth. Soon after there is **The Emperor- IV**: it represents stability, respect of the rules and the ability to listen to our fellow men. It reminds us of a family father and tells us never to use other people. After the Emperor we have **The Pope- V**: it's a sign connecting the material to the spiritual word, a Pontifex, that's it. This card warns us to follow our heart and never to give up to temptation. That's why it's in opposition with the Arcane number XV, *The Devil*. But let's follow the order; after The Pope there are **The Lovers- VI**: we are all made of two opposite sides, male and female, positive and negative. We must accept also our shadowy sides and confide in other people, it's the symbol of new relationships coming.

Moving further there's **The Cart-VII**: it obviously refers to travelling. You see, the image is that of a coach drawn by two horses. The journey represented could be our soul's journey on the Earth, so the Cart will represent our body, the means which we need to live. The card can also foretell the choices we are going to take in a short time, we might afford some extremely uncertain moments. It's no accident that two horses are represented, the number "two" reminds us that we always have different choices. The next Major Arcana is **Justice-VIII:** this one always urges us to uphold our ideas and to act having a full faith in ourselves. We have to find peace and harmony. If we go on we find **The Hermit-IX**: it underlines how we sometimes need to be alone to find a light, which means wisdom. The card is usually represented by an elderly person holding a lantern in his hand, the symbol of intuition and knowledge, and in the other a stick, the means to overcome the troubles of life. It could be considered as the young man in the first card, **The Crazy**, having grown up and with a wider knowledge. If we move further we get to the **Wheel of fortune-X**: it's the symbol of fate, of the wheel of our life turning in spite of our will. The condition of mankind is not unalterable, it's continually changing. Our true lightness is often to have the ability to let ourselves be dragged by events. We find soon after **The Force-XI**: our adult side, the one which has to guide us. We must never hide our emotions, but follow them instead. We don't have to tame the lion by cruelty, but by our will and wisdom; the lion represents our instincts. We can often find Force and Justice in the opposite order, that's Force at number VIII and Justice at number XI. In the following position there's **The Hangman-XII:** someone who looks at the world from a different point of view. It could be considered as the moment of "reflection break" leading us to Illumination. Its roots, the feet, point upwards, to the sky, reminding us that we come from the Divine, from something above us. Going on we run into the card we fear the most, **Death-XIII**: it means the end of a period and the beginning of a new one. That's part of our life, it's not always something negative. We must be able to throw away what has become useless in our spiritual growth. In the next place there is **Temperance-XIV:** it foretells a period of quietness, full of harmony. Moderation leads to peace of mind. This means that the phases of peace and rest are necessary to recharge ourselves.

We then find **The Devil-XV**: this card reminds us that the souls descended into the material world and that we are always being tempted. In certain phases in our life, the force of our selfishness brings to light the hidden sides of our Ego, those sides we try to hide from everybody, including ourselves. What the Devil represents is just that: the tempting Ego, our material side which makes us heavier and prevents us from being uplifted. We have to know and to face evil if we want to gain awareness and become better. Taking the decision of becoming incarnate on the Earth is not easy. Let's go on to **The Tower-XVI**: the sudden collapse of a situation. Destruction was necessary to open doors to something different and new; this card will make us understand that unfortunately nothing is eternal.

The next Arcane are **The Stars-XVII**: a new phase of life starts with them, characterized by inspiration and creativity. Starlight makes our wishes brighter.

After the Stars, there's **The Moon-XVIII**: the interpretation of this card is that something mysterious and unknown can interfere with our intuition and deceive us. Nourishing our wishes in the shadow and acting shrewdly is better, to avoid becoming the target of envy. After the Moon and the Stars, here's **The Sun-XIX**: this card wants to tell us that obstacles have been overcome.

The Sun represents a moment in life characterized by a strong positive energy and by success. It is usually drawn as a child because, after a long journey to discover ourselves again, we have reached Knowledge and we feel like light-hearted children. We're almost coming to the end. The next card is **Judgment- XX**: our soul has woken up, we're wearing new clothes. We've learnt to look into ourselves to find the truth again and to get free from prejudices. Let's finish with **The world-XXI** at last: a cycle is coming to an end, we're going to be rewarded for our hard work. New opportunities are looming up on the horizon.

You see, these are in a few words the Major Arcana of the Tarots. They are wonderful, aren't they? The most important thing is to be able to look at them, the figures can speak. Let's have a break now,

I'm having a glass of wine, which is never bad, and then I'll go on, if you wish…"

"We don't want to make you tired, Stella", my sister claimed with fondness.

"Absolutely not! I'm pleased that you are being so attentive. Will you let Anne and Alison read your notes too, if they ask you?"

"Of course. If they ask me…but I doubt that, my sister isn't interested in things like these."

That wasn't true, I had been listening to everything Stella had explained, I just pretended to be indifferent. I feared other people's judgment.

"What are you talking about over there?", my mum intruded.

"About Tarots, Rebecca. Do you know them?" Stella had finished her glass of wine and she was ready to start again.

"Cards? No, I don't know them…And what about you Sarah, are you taking notes?"

"Yes, mum, I love these things, they're really interesting."

"If you found your maths lessons interesting too, you would have passed your last *SAT* better."

"Oh, you're so boring, Rebecca. Even on Christmas day. Let her alone", my granny spoke kindly.

"That's the truth, mum. By the way, Mal and Tom are discussing football now, so I'll join you if I don't bother you."

"You're welcome. You know, I was taking for granted that your mum could read the cards and was a *wiccan*, but not all women who make ointments, herbal teas and follow the moon phases are like that, I can understand", Stella told her, arranging her long red skirt to sit down more comfortably on the armchair.

"What?"

"A *wiccan*!", granny answered.

"And what's that?"

"It's a new- pagan religion, as I was telling Stella, I studied it and I know it very well, but…I'm a solitary witch, I've never attended congregations nor have I received any initiation."

"Are you a witch, granny?", Sarah turned suddenly, her eyes opened wide were showing all her wonder.

"I usually define witches as women working with Nature, respecting it and living in harmony with its cycles. What's more, by meditating and getting to know myself, I can understand what I should change or improve in my life and in other people's lives.

The word *witch* comes from *wise*. Witches use in fact their wisdom to reach their goal."

"Am I going to be like that too?"

"I'll tell you a secret: all women are like that, but not all of them know they are…Just follow your instinct and live in harmony with Nature's cycles, that's the only way to understand what is the right path for you", she told her fondly, caressing her shoulder.

"And now, dear Stella, we're all ears: if you wish, show us the Minor Arcana."

"I'm not going to explain all of them one by one, since they're fifty-six cards, or we'll be still here on New Year's day! What's more, when I read my cards I only use the Major ones. I'm going to tell you just the meaning of the four suits: wands, cups, spades and diamonds. So, **Wands** are connected to the element Fire, they stand for energy and creative will, as if a spark was falling on us, starting the process of creation, an inspiration turned into something practical. **Cups** remind us of Water, they are linked to emotions. The spark has opened a passage, so ideas pour inside it, just like water. **Spades**, the air element, foretell some trouble, but we can protect ourselves, we can build our own reality. **Diamonds** are the Earth, cosmic powers become material, they are the symbols of welfare and creation.

All the cards, for each seed, have numbers going from one to seven and four figures: Infantryman, Knight, Queen and King.

If we want to read them, we have to consider their position, which are the cards next to them and above all what they're arousing into us. Interpreting the Tarots is not simple, my secret is just to observe them and let myself be dragged by what they're telling my heart… did you like them, Rebecca?"

"I was just having a look at the images on the Major Arcana, they're so beautiful! You found such delicious drawings. One of my childhood friends used to collect different packs, she had twenty of them at least." My mum was staring at them one by one with curiosity. "And now", she went on, " why don't you try to tell me how will things go with my new activity in Reading?"

"I'm sorry dear, I'm very tired, I can't focus in the right way…I'll do it another time, ok? I'm sure things will be great for you." Stella was clearly worn out. She hadn't been undergoing chemotherapy cycles for a while, but she still got easily tired.

"Don't worry, I was just curious", our mum comforted her.

"Alison and I are starting to get back home…"

"No, Stella, I've got a room ready for you, I'm not going to let you drive to Newbury. Just stay here and I'm going to make a good porridge for breakfast, or do you prefer scrambled eggs?"

"Oh, thanks Susan, but we…"

"No trouble, you'll be my guests."

We all spent the night at the cottage, that was real Christmas magic.

V.

The power of officinal plants

I could never have imagined I was going to love our new life in Reading so much.

Sonning Common was a delicious residential neighbourhood, we could get to the centre in a few minutes. Alison was in our class and my parents' cafeteria in Duke Street, next to the *Oracle*, the shopping centre, went immediately booming.

We were on our last but one year at secondary school, we were going to be fifteen in May.

My sister was absolutely the most courted girl in the school, and I didn't mind that. She had left her absent-minded girlish look, she had become an intriguing and mysterious girl. That was probably the reason why she looked so charming, along with her blonde hair and her doe eyes. She didn't talk much and she was often lost in her thoughts.

Alison and I didn't care about boys instead, or the truth is, we didn't have time for them. We spent all our free time at the riding school, horses had become by then our greatest passion. Our parents had decided to buy a dog for us, we had called it Ridge, it was a peaceful and joyful Golden Retriever that made my days full. I was sure I would study as a vet when I grew up.

I wanted to devote myself to horses all my life.

I visited granny only one weekend a month, my sister kept visiting her every week instead.

She got up every Saturday morning and went shopping at the *Oracle* or at *Primark*; she then stopped at my mum and dad's cafeteria, where a *double vegan cappuccino* was waiting for her, she headed to the station and she got to Marlow in less than an hour.

"You're as a creature of habit as a cat", I told her every time and she always answered I should go with her too, because granny was always asking her about me and she longed to see me, she also underlined the fact that, if I wished to ride, there were Mal's horses.

Smelly and *Shelly* had unfortunately died, he now had *Grumpy* and *Jumpy.*

"Ok, I'll come next weekend, I promise you."

I missed the cottage, it was my second home, especially the garden, but I had to get ready for competitions, handle Ridge and study.

As I had promised, I visited granny with Sarah the following weekend.

We found her at the kitchen counter, surrounded by dried herbs and small jugs. Kiki was crunching on a chair, but it started rubbing against Sarah's legs as soon as it heard her come in, just like it used to do when we were children. It was almost ten years old, but granny pampered it so much, it would live ten years more.

"Here you are, girls! Just in time: I've just finished filtering and bottling my tinctures and herbal infused oils". One of our granny's greatest passions was .to work with herbs and officinal plants; she got it from her mother too. "Look, Mal has bought a labelling machine for me, isn't that fantastic? The hawthorn tincture is ready for you, Sarah; Anna, here is your St. John's wort to make infusions and I made an oil for your mum, to tone up her breast, arms and buttocks…it's never too early to take care of oneself."

Since we had our first menstrual period when we were twelve, granny had started helping us with her "brews", as I called them. I must admit they were very useful though.

Sarah had trouble to fall asleep, especially with waxing moon, which was our pre-menstrual phase, but when she took some drops of hawthorn tincture, she could sleep well.

She had advised me to drink St. John's wort infusions every evening, she said it helped my mood. She always sent mum something for her body care. Mum was thirty-five, she was still a very beautiful woman, but she showed her tiredness, since she stood on her feet all day long at work.

"How are my little girls? Mal might come for lunch. Sit down, I'll make you a sandwich. I'm sorry I haven't had time to cook today, I have been working hard among tinctures, small bags and oils." Her hair was gathered up, she was wearing a pink apron and she was very good humored as usual. How she managed, I've never known.

"If you teach us to make herbal oils, we can help you, or we can do them ourselves...is it difficult?", my sister suggested enthusiastically.

"It's not difficult, darling, but like for anything else, you have to know what you're doing and follow some simple rules. I think you've grown up enough to learn to do everything. Anna, are you interested in it?"

"Since I'm here, I can listen too...", I said in a dull voice, without showing the least enthusiasm. I was never going to admit that I would like to learn everything our granny had to teach us. It was an ancient knowledge; there was an aura of mystery in everything she did, filtering and bottling wasn't all, there was something more and that made me curious.

"Sarah, do you still have your notebook?"

"It must be in the bedroom upstairs, I'll go and fetch it."

As soon as Kiki saw her move away, it lifted its small muzzle questioningly, then it went back lazing quietly on its chair; I had always been jealous of the attentions it devoted exclusively to my sister, I meant nothing to it.

"Cats are strange, Anne, don't bother about it. It's fond of her."

Granny was always able to read my thoughts.

"It probably smells Ridge's odour", she went on.

"No, granny, it was like that also before I got my dog: as if I was invisible for it. It hurt me when I was a child, not now, but I can't understand what's up in its mind."
"What's up in a cat's mind? Understanding their thoughts is really impossible, they follow their liking, that's all. Thank God it doesn't scratch you. Do you know that it keeps spitting at Mrs. Bray, every time it sees her? My naughty Kiki, but it keeps me good company by the way!"
"Do you feel lonely?", I asked her getting curious.
"Luckily I don't even have time to feel lonely, my dear. The secret is, to find always something to do…"
"Here I am, granny. We're ready." Sarah arrived with her pink notebook, I used to make fun of her for when I was a child.
"Excellent, so: let's start at once by saying that I make herbal infused oils and tinctures at home, besides infusions and small bags. I use mainly my own plants and the ones Mal finds out, or the ones people offer me. For example, St. John's wort gets here already dried up by a dear friend who lives in Italy. All plants have special qualities, both on a healing and on an energetic level, but you already know that…For my oils, I generally use dried up plants, excepting some of them like hyperic, arnica and lemon balm. I wash them, I let them dry up carefully laying them on a cloth, I mince them roughly, I put them into a jug, the ones for jam are perfect, and I cover them with oil. I always use sunflower seeds oil, because it doesn't cover the smell, olive oil is too strong according to my taste; sweet almond oil is nourishing and cheap, but its fault is that it releases a very pungent smell if it turns rancid. I personally never use precise amounts of oil, the most important thing is to cover the whole content. I then let the jug rest in the dark for twenty-eight days and I shake it every two days. At the end of maceration time, I start filtering: I let the oil fall into a clean jug, I press the herbs too and I let it rest for some time more. After that, I go on to the second filtering and, helping myself with a sterilized gauze, I put the oil

into a dark jug, if you can find the ones with a dropper they are really perfect.

For tinctures, instead, herbs must macerate in some watered down alcohol, not in oil. It's difficult to find alcohol in our country, they don't sell it at the supermarket. You have to go to an *off-licence*: I go to an Italian shop in Maidenhead and I buy the typical alcohol for cakes, it's very expensive but it lasts for a long time."

She looked at us, to understand if we were following her, then she went on, "You can't make tinctures with all plants, however. Let's make some examples. **Lavender**: it's a fantastic plant, who doesn't like its delicate smell? It protects from evil and helps to sleep peacefully. You can certainly remember when I rubbed you with it when you were children, you in particular, Anne, and I told you the nursery rhyme my grandmother used to tell me: *"With lavender oil and the Moon in the sky, may my little girl sleep peacefully tonight!"* Because plants, candles and stones have just half of their effect without our will's power! My granny taught me that too… Where was I? Ah, yes, our lavender, it helps to reduce anxiety, if we just look at it, we feel more peaceful. It's absolutely fantastic. The oil is perfect for the skin, just put a drop of it on a cotton wad and pad your face with it, to wipe any impurity away. I use it for my headache when I feel tired, I keep a gauze soaked in fresh water and some oil drops on my forehead. You can also drink the infusion, it has anti-depression powers: 15-30gr of dried flowers in one litre of boiling water, left in infusion for ten minutes. It's very easy! For the tincture you must use instead alcohol for cakes at 95°: six and a half cups of alcohol and three and a half cups of water in a jar to cover the lavender flowers, then you close it. They must be left to macerate for twenty-eight days, the jar must be shaken every day, then you filter it all: you throw away the flowers, while the liquid part you get will be our tincture. The jar must be kept in the dark. You can use four drops four times a day, or sixteen drops in an infusion in the evening. It's a useful remedy against intestinal troubles, nausea, sickness and when you feel nervous, anxious and stressed for work."

I looked around me and I withdrew my attention from granny's words for a moment: her kitchen was wide, with a large glass-window opening directly on the garden, and a small back door to get to it. Mum kept telling her she should change all that, because the furniture was old, but granny liked it just the way it was. There was a big table in the middle where she cooked and got her "brews" ready, she had placed Kiki's armchair next to the stove and there was a corner devoted to plant drying, she had stretched two strings and she hang there upside down bundles of plants all summer long. "Ah, I forgot", she went on. "To produce herbal oiles , the maceration time must be always from two to four weeks. I like making them with waxing Moon, maybe on the day before full Moon and wait for all the Moon cycle. With some herbs it's better to put the jugs in sunlight, so the process gets faster, but this is not appropriate with delicate plants. Another herb I often use is **Mint**: it's refreshing, energizing and invigorating, it's very useful against the sense of heat, heavy legs and when you feel tired. Mint can help you to overcome a feeling of inferiority, in the form of incense it purifies the house, keeps evil spirits away and makes money revenues easier. When I work with mint, I always keep saying: *"Mint, mint, bring me everything I want, till there is nothing more!"* You can certainly oil candles with herbal oils too. Sarah, do you remember when I told you that it's a good rule to oil them before using them? That's useful to impress our will and to protect them. Mint isn't very strong here in England, we pick it up at the end of June, it dries fast, just in three days. I give a double maceration to my oils: I put the dried leaves into a jag, I cover them with my usual seeds oil, I close it and I leave it to rest for fourteen days, shaking it every two. I filter it for the first time after two weeks, I use the filtered oil once more to cover some fresh leaves instead, I leave them to macerate two weeks more, I filter all that for the last time

and my essential ointment will be ready! If you prefer a stronger smell, you can add three drops of mint essence. I don't make essential oils, only herbal infused ones. Mint tincture is made instead letting it macerate in three and a half cups of alcohol at 95° and three and a half cups of water, the process is the same: everything is kept closed in a jag for twenty-height days. You can use thirty drops diluted in water twice-three times a day. It's useful for bad digestion, but also for light bronchitis, sinusitis, cystitis, car sickness and so on…"
"You've got a small mint plant, haven't you granny?"
"Of course, it grows easily, it's even very infesting, it's better to put it in a vase on its own or in a separate lawn."
Granny got up and started wandering around the kitchen, lunch time was coming.
"Let's go on to my beloved **Rose**: do you know that each colour has a different meaning? The red ones are connected to love, the pink ones to friendship, the violet to mourning, the white to the care of emotions and the yellow stands for jealousy,,, Her thorns are excellent protection amulets. It's a plant which brings good luck and it also attracts fairies (as people say). To make our oil, we must chose a strong smelling flower, usually the Damask rose. You must use only fresh flowers and change them every three days, till you get the perfume you're looking for. Then you must filter it and the day after you must suck up the water balls made by using fresh petals."
"Why can't we use dried up petals?"
"Because they don't have any smell, Anne. You get in this way an oil which can improve your self-esteem and your patience, which keeps away negative thoughts and depression and brings a bit of joy. If you rub it on your skin, it soothes irritation and reduces wrinkles, it helps also against menstrual pains if you put it directly on your belly. It's also a very famous aphrodisiac, but you shouldn't be interested in that…or should you maybe? Do you have any boyfriend yet?"

"No!", we answered at the same time.

"There would be nothing wrong, girls!"

"I think all boys are silly. I prefer spending my days going horse-riding!", I burst out with determination.

"Has anybody caught your attention at the riding school?"

"I don't care, granny…" That wasn't absolutely true. I had lost my head over Liam, my twenty-four -years -old instructor, but that was just Platonic love, he was nine years older than me, and that was certainly too much. I always tried to do my best in competitions, just to make an impression on him, that made me one of the best and it was enough for me.

"And what about you, Sarah?"

"Oh, Sarah always gets lots of red roses at school", I made fun of her.

"I don't like any boy…"

"Neither Bob?", I went on.

Bob was a very attractive boy, he was 1.80 metres tall, with green eyes, freckles, a cover-smile and besides all that, he would be the perfect guy for my sister, if only she had been a less solitary girl. He was the typical good boy, he didn't smoke, he didn't even drink Pimm's, he had excellent marks at school and, above all, he was damn rich. He had been courting her wildly for ages, but she had never agreed to go out with him.

"I don't even care about Bob at the moment!", she claimed loftily.

"At the moment? Are you going to wait till he is eighty?"

Granny burst out laughing. " What's holding you up, Sarah? You could go and have a walk along the Thames, it's so romantic."

I didn't find it romantic at all, with all those ducks doing their business everywhere. It might be romantic in London, but not so much in Reading.

"I sincerely consider having a boyfriend as a waste of time, that's all."

"You're the oddest fifteen-years-old girls I've ever met. Just two gorgeous spinsters!", our granny's laughter was like a contagious volcano of energy.

"What are you laughing at, wonderful girls?"

"Mal!"

"Come in, Mal. I was just going to make a good sandwich for the girls, would you like one to? What about ham and cheddar?"

"I could never give up Susan's famous sandwiches. So, what are your plans for the weekend?"

"We were having a lesson about herbs and officinal plants…By the way, I made the dandelion tincture for you, it's over there, near the window, help yourself and remember: 50 drops in little water three times a day before or far from meals. Let's go back to ourselves, girls, do you know what dandelion is? That flower which loses its tuft into the air if you blow on it and which makes your wishes come true, if you are able to take it off all at once. It was a very beautiful yellow flower at first, very ordinary in all fields, since it grows wild. It stands for the transience of human life for me: the flower lasts for a very short time, just one or two days usually, and a simple breath of wind is enough to bring it away.

All that should make us think about the shortness of the things we own and of our existence: everything we have and we see around us will finish sooner or later, or will change into something else at least.

By the way, dandelion has strong purifying powers, it helps our liver and kidneys to get rid more easily of the waste we have accumulated."

"That's true. Your granny's tincture helped me a lot with my bile duct inflammation", Mal said, fumbling about the stove to increase the heat. It was incredible how he moved at ease in granny's house.

"You can also make a decoction to get purified after parties: you have to let a spoonful of dandelion root boil in three cups of water for ten minutes."

"Have you already spoken with the girls about our idea of taking them to Glastonbury?" Mal was always very enthusiastic when he could do trips out of town, since he didn't have many opportunities for that.

"No, I hadn't told them yet, you did at the moment. Girls, how about coming with us to Glastonbury?"

"Of course, granny!"

"For the festival?"

"I'd rather avoid the festival period, actually, Anne, there's such a mess. We could go as soon as school ends."

"After we come back from Palma..." We still used to go to the Balearic Islands and visit our grand-parents every summer. They lived in Magaluf at the time, not in the town centre anymore, because they missed England (as they used to say) and that was certainly the most similar neighbourhood to our country, at least as far as pubs and drunk young people were concerned...

"That's perfect, we are going in August then. It's gone! I'm really looking forward to showing you the village I grew up in. I wonder if I can still climb to the *Tor*."

"What's the *Tor*, granny?"

"It's a hill just out of town, there's a tower with no roof on top. A church was built there, but it was a place devoted to the pagan worship of the Goddess Mother in the pre-roman age. At the foot of the hill there are *Chalice Well's* gardens, were the very famous well can be found, whose name refers to the chalice, the Mother's womb; the *Tor* on the hill is instead considered as the Goddess's breast, people walk up there on a sort of pilgrimage to get support and protection. When we are on the spot, I'll explain it better. Sarah, my dear, before you forget, take your **Hawthorn** tincture, I put it on the shelf at the entrance."

"Are you having fun with your new labelling machine, Susan?", Mal joked.

"It's very useful, thanks."

"Going back to what we were saying, what do we need Hawthorn for? To sleep well?" my sister asked between morsels. How much she ate was incredible, since she was always so thin; I was slightly shorter than her and I had softer curves.

"Yes, Sarah, hawthorn helps you sleep. You know, you just have to take fifteen drops before going to bed now, but when you grow older, you'll need thirty drops. The tincture can be made by macerating the dried up flowers in seven cups of alcohol and three cups of water. The flowers should be picked up only on *May Day*, because people believe the plant is the home of fairies and they let us pick them up just on that magic day. I like it because it's a symbol of hope, the flowers foretell the arrival of the good season." Granny had always had a preference for that celebration at the start of May.

"People once used hawthorn as a natural fence", Mal went on, "You know, to bound their lands. That's why you can often find it next to the house doors; its thorns protect us, or people used to say it at least."

"That's true. Its thorns, like those of roses, were used to make protective talismans. But let's stop talking now, I'm going to have a good cheddar sandwich too."

Sarah and I studied after lunch, while our granny was finishing her knitting and old Mal was having a nap on the armchair. There was an unreal silence around the house, broken only by the clicking of the knitting needles; that strange feeling was always hovering there, as if we were in a parallel world and ordinary life was light years far away.

"Let's have a break, girls. I'll make tea." There was always a good pretext for an *Earl Grey*.

"I didn't finish to explain my oils to you before", granny went on, holding a piping hot cup in her hands, "I forgot to tell you that you can keep an oil only up to two years, but my advice is just one year, and you can put a rosemary branch in it as an anti-oxidizing, but that could cover most of the sweet smell. You can make oils with almost any herbs you wish. The **Pot Marigold** one is excellent, it's very useful on dry or chapped skins, it helps to soothe the pain coming from rhagades and irritations, like the ones from babies nappies, and it alleviates the itch after insect bites. On an energetic level it instead makes decisions easier: whenever I have any doubts about a choice I should make, I take a cotton wad, I dampen it in pot marigold oil, I wrap it in a cloth, I put it under my pillow and I sleep on it all night long. I always get up the day after well decided about what to do.

A friend of mine makes an excellent **Sage** oil, she says it helps money gain, she usually puts some drops of oil on banknotes. She's never had financial troubles since I met her, so it obviously works. But Sage has got other qualities: it's sweet smelling, so it's a very good deodorizer, it reduces perspiration, it makes superficial wounds heal and it also has a strong depurative power.

Take a spoon of honey with two drops of this oil, it's a good natural remedy against food poisoning, stomach ache, diarrhoea and the after-effects of intestinal infections."

"Alison's mum always burns it."

"Of course, burning sage in the house wipes away negative forces which build up in the rooms. I often do it as well: coarse salt in the corners, under the doormat and sage smoke. Many people come and go in this house, they come here to give vent to their feelings, to ask me for help and just to have a little talk. I can't keep other people's energy in the house, I could fall ill. I remember a woman used to come here, her name was Helen and I didn't like her at all."

"So why did you let her in?"

"She was a friend's friend, I didn't want to be rude. Her voice was enough to make me nervous, I felt sick when we were in the same room. Kiki didn't like her too, it always hid under the bed when she came in. Can you remember her, Mal? Mal?"

"Mmm…what?" he was still having his nap.

"Do you remember Helen? The blonde one…"

"Of course, I have bought you the broom for Imbolc since then."

"What does the broom have to do with that?"

"Well, you see Anne, the **broom** is a powerful protection, and what's more, it's a symbol connected with witches. Putting one on the house door, for instance, will protect you from evil eyes and spells, they get imprisoned in the bristles. If you leave it upside down, it wipes away gossip. Mal always gives me one at Imbolc, because that's the period of the year devoted to cleaning, people get purified and throw away the waste, just like dirt. When you use it to clean the house, it doesn't need to touch the floor directly, visualizing it in your mind is enough, so negative astral accumulation will fly away. The broomstick is usually made of ash, it's a protective tree, the fibres are made of purifying birch, tied up by a willow branch, that's a sacred tree for the Goddess. But with Helen, neither cleaning with the broom, nor burning sage was enough!"

"I've already told you, Susan: Helen and you had met in a past life and she obviously hadn't treated you well. You still carry those scars in your soul."

"How did you manage to push her away in the end, granny?"

"I tried at first with the "four thieves' vinegar", then with a sort of nettle oil, which I call "Hecate's oil.""

"What are they?"

"Mal, can you explain the girls "the four thieves vinegar", since it's you who invented it?"

"I didn't invent it, I've been producing it for ages. My poor wife taught me." Mal had lost his wife just a few years after their marriage, they didn't have children and he had been alone since then, satisfied with the deep fondness linking himself to our granny. They might make a wonderful couple!

"People say that in the seventeenth century, while Black death was raging all other Europe, there was a group of four thieves in France who always succeeded in robbing the plague –stricken houses without ever falling ill. Those thieves were once caught and they decided to avoid death penalty by telling the secret which had kept them safe till then. They said that, before each robbery, they washed their bodies and soaked their cloths in a certain vinegar, where various herbs and antiseptic plants had been macerated, like sage, rosemary, mint, lavender and angelica.

That recipe became very famous at once, and everyone started to use it on house walls, furniture and clothes. However, it seems that the original plants were actually four: laurel, lavender, sage and thyme; this is the recipe I usually follow. Since luckily today Black Death isn't threatening us anymore, people use it to make their hair stronger and as an antidandruff, but also to wipe away dirt.

What's more, because of its antiseptic qualities, it's very useful to wash dog hair and to prevent viral and epidermis illnesses in men.

It had been finally noticed that, when it's sprayed in certain rooms, if you focus very well on the goal you want to get to, this compound can push away anything harmful hiding there, granting protection to the house and the work spaces. It is therefore used in modern esotericism to get rid of people troubling our balance, like Helen did for your grandmother."

"I still use it, it's fantastic: but Helen was such a tough nut to crack! So I invented a new kind of **nettle** oil: the pre-eminently protection plant, connected to Mars and to the fire element, it's the ideal one for defence. Its qualities are very detoxifying, tonic, invigorating and anti-inflammation, it's a real wonder. As it's very stinging, you certainly need to use gloves when picking it up: the irritating substances contained in its hair can be eliminated by cooking it. I added to its oil: mint, rosemary, willow, myrrh, cinnamon, St. John's wort, anise, ginger, rose, red wine, garlic, pepper and some ashes from my fireplace. I made it on the first wining moon Tuesday summoning Hecate to protect me. Every time Helen came here, I kept a black obsidian on the table and I sprayed a candle with that oil, lighting it before her. I always felt anxious, but things went better. I tried to visualize her far from me. After a while she told me she couldn't come anymore, because she was going to move to

Briton, and I've never heard of her anymore. Mission accomplished, that's incredible! Mal and I celebrated the news by going to the pub."

"But what did she do to you?"

"Nothing, Anne. I must admit she was always very kind to me. The problem was, she irradiated a natural negativity, or I felt she was a threat at least. I've already told you, I felt scared if I only heard her voice. You can sometimes meet people like that, they appear to be harmless, but they lack harmony with our energy field. They are uncommon, luckily."

"So, why did you summon Hecate? Who 's she?"

"It's very difficult to explain who Hecate is, Sarah…It's a goddess. She stands for wining moon. If we compare the moon cycle to a person's life, waxing moon stands for youth, fool moon is adulthood, wining moon is old age and black moon is death. Young girl-mother- crone, Hecate lived all the three phases of life. An elderly person is wise and knows what is right. I usually summon her just to have justice, clearness and protection. She's the goddess of forks, of crossroads: in the past people could find statues representing her at crossroads. They thought she could help people to choose the path they would follow. Her most important quality is omniscience: she can see the past, the present and the future of us all. Just for that quality she's considered as a symbol of the link between everybody's past and future lives. She's represented in classical iconography holding a book in one hand and a torchlight in the other, as symbols of her knowledge and wisdom. The connection between Hecate and witchcraft could come from the fact she was considered as having the power of making people's wishes come true or not, and of influencing their birth and the ones of animals and plants. Hecate was associated with the moon, especially with the dark phase of the satellite, while Artemis stood for the waxing phase and Selene for the bright phase on full moon day. A was sitting in the garden on a summer evening, I was wondering about how I could solve my troubles with Helen. I didn't want her in my house anymore, but I didn't know what to do. I heard an owl at that moment, it was on the willow tree, on the other side of the road. I kept listening to it and I then naturally associated the night animal with Hecate. I understood I had to work in mutual understanding with her: the nettle oil came to my mind and I made it. Let's say I got a sign."

"It might have been a simple chance, I would have told her simply not to come anymore and that's all; without wasting any more time", I ended brusquely.

"I actually agree with you for once, Anne."

Mal at least luckily agreed with me.

"I had no excuse to prevent her from coming: she was just looking for a little company two hours a week."

"She should have bought a dog or joined a club!" That was my opinion.

"My dear Susan, the truth is you're too kind and she was absorbing your energy. She felt well when she visited you, you always have something to teach, your house is welcoming. Without forgetting that your *scones* are the best all over England!"

"You're right when you say that she was absorbing my energy. I felt terribly weak when she went away."

"Was she doing it on purpose?"

"No, Sarah, she didn't realize that; she knew nothing about energy. Her conversation was frivolous. She was long- winded and extremely superficial. That's finished, by the way. I'll know how to defend myself, if I ever meet someone like her again. But let's talk about something lighter now. I've never told you what kind of oil I make for your mum…"

"Ok, so I can fall asleep on the armchair once more. That's women's talk!"

"No, Mal, I have to ask you a favour. Could you kindly go and fetch some wood to light the fireplace? Night is coming. I was telling you…I make an oil based on **Borage** for your mum. Do you know it?"

"No, I don't even know what it looks like", I admitted sincerely.

"It's a small blue flower, with a star- like shape, they appear in the summer along the roads or in uncultivated fields. It's better to pick our herbs always far from traffic areas. You can use the flower tops, the leaves and the juicy stalks, picked up when the blossoming has just started. They can be used fresh or dried up. On an energetic level, it helps to fight depression, it's an excellent remedy against sadness. A borage decoction is the ideal against bronchitis and cold. I used to make it when you were children. You must put fifteen gr. of borage, possibly fresh, in one litre of boiling water for ten minutes and then drink two or three cups a day. The decoction is for external use in the form of compress against acne, reddened skin or cutaneous rash due to rubella or scarlet fever. The oil is used instead to tone up breasts, arms and bottoms. I make a borage oil, using dried flowers, leaves and seeds; I put them in my usual seed oil to macerate for twenty-eight days. I make an oil of dried daisies at the same time and I then mix the two oils. With that recipe, I get much better results than the ones granted by the most modern and advertised creams, without any of their side effects. It must be spread with small circular massages, with an open hand, on the breast before going to bed. I hope your mother does it. Devoting some time to our personal care is very important. I sent Mal to fetch some wood, so he couldn't hear our secrets…"

"So, do you usually use it too, granny?"

"Of course, Anne. I'm seventy-five, I'm not so old, I can still take care of my beauty."

She could certainly do it very well, she had just a few wrinkles and her hair was still thick and bright red, highlighted by her green eyes. She was a gorgeous seventy-five-old woman.

It was particularly cold that night, it was February. A strong wind was blowing from the north, making strange noises against the sash windows.

"Anne, I can't sleep…", Sarah told me in the middle of the night.

"Have you taken your drops?"

"No, I left them downstairs."

"So, go and take them!"

"I'm cold, I don't want to get out of my bed."

"So, just stay there and sleep will come…"

"Can't you go and fetch them?"

"What makes you think I feel like doing it?"

"If you don't go, I will keep talking all night long!"

"So I'll put my earphones on!"

"Please, Anne…"

"Ok, but you own me a favour."

I crawled downstairs wrapped in my dressing gown, avoiding carefully to fall from the stairs.

"Why did you get up?"

"You scared me, granny! I'm going to fetch Sarah's hawthorn drops, because she can't sleep…And what are you doing here?"

"I was just checking I had closed the back door after Mal had gone, otherwise this bad wind will make it slam."

"Why doesn't Mal ever sleep here?"

"Because he has a home on his own, I don't understand why he should stay here!"

"Oh, granny, let's go…you're such a nice couple!"

"We are a couple of old friends…that's all! Each one in his home. Let's go and bring your sister the hawthorn, if we don't want to spend the night awake."

We found Sarah trembling under the quilt.

"I'm so cold!"

"It's not so cold, the radiators are working. Let me see, you're burning, poor child! You've got fever. Let me see if I still have some

Calpol here.

"We don't use *Calpol* anymore, granny, mum usually gives us *Nurofen.*"

"No *Nurofen*, I don't keep many medicines luckily. No problem, that means I'll make a good herbal tea for you. You're staying in bed and Mal and I are taking you home tomorrow morning."

"I'm sorry, granny."

"Why? It's not your fault, my dear."

"Just try not to pass on fever to me, I have to train for my competitions. I can't afford not going to the riding school."

"Anne, don't be so rude with your sister!"

"I'm serious, I don't want to fall ill for her fault."

"So you'll drink my "health tea" too, it can't harm you."

"How do you make it?", I asked worried.

" I boil a clove of garlic, a dried chilly-pepper, three laurel leaves and a cinnamon stick. I let it boil for twenty minutes at least. I then add half a squeezed lemon, two honey spoons and three concentrated ginger drops."

"Oh, my God, I'm feeling sick!"

"Don't be silly, it's good and healthy."

Granny came back half an hour later with three sweet smelling, piping hot cups.

"Here you are, I'm having a cup too, to keep you company."

It wasn't bad, it tasted really strong, but it was pleasant after all.

"I thought it would be worse, to tell the truth", I confessed.

"Have you seen, Anne? You should trust me! How are you, Sarah?"

"I'm bad, my temperature is rising."

"That's normal. Be quiet now, the hot tea is going to help you. Don't worry, we are going to *Boots* tomorrow to buy medicines, then we're going home. Try to rest now. Good night, girls."

"Night, granny."

I couldn't sleep well, the wind kept blowing hard and Sarah kept moaning in her sleep.

Kiki's miaowling woke me up the next morning, it probably claimed its food or its morning cuddles.

Granny had already got up. She slept very little, she loved getting up early in the morning, seeing dawn and working at the cooker.

She was talking on the phone, probably with my mum.

I could hear her say things like that: they must learn to dry their hair well and to wear warmer clothes… Mum always scolded us too when she saw us going out with damp hair or too light t-shirts.

Mal came in after a while, with his happy voice and his cheerfulness filling the whole house, together with our granny's crystal laughter.

"Anne, come downstairs, breakfast is ready!"

Porridge with honey and currants, my favourite since ever.

"Is Sarah sleeping?"

"Unless she's dead…"

"Silly girl!"

"She has been moaning all night long…she didn't leave me have rest."

"I've already told your mother. As soon as she gets up, we'll take you to Reading."

"That's great, I'm going to spend Sunday alone at home with my dying sister…"

VI.

Persecutions

As foreseen, I fell ill too in two days' time. My mum didn't have any laurel leaves nor cinnamon sticks at home, to make me the famous "health tea". In spite of my granny's phone scolding, she found it faster to go to *Boots* and buy me some paracetamol, which she integrated with some laurel oil drops bought at *Holland & Barrett*: they tasted awfully, but granny had insisted so much on making me take them three times a day at least. I couldn't go neither to school nor even less horse riding, and the worse was I was going to stay at home the following week for our half term holidays. I asked my parents if I could stay in Reading instead of going to granny's, I was almost fifteen by the time, there would be nothing wrong in spending my days by myself. Of course Sarah didn't agree with me, but we found a good compromise: I could stay half the week at home and in the other half I would join my sister in Marlow. We had to make a history paper about the Holy Inquisition, especially about heretics and witches persecutions.
Our work team was composed of: Sarah, Alison, Tom, Harry and I, of course. The girls should find out the reasons, the boys the most violent side: torture and questioning. I didn't like working in a team, I preferred when I could seldom write by myself.

"But why did the Catholic church do all that, granny? I don't understand…"
"Oh, Sarah, there are so many things in history which can't be explained!", our grandmother moralized, sitting on her armchair with a cup of tea in her hand and Kiki crouching at her feet.
We had decided to involve her too, to make our history paper ready,

her knowledge could be helpful for us. Alison was joining us on Friday; we were going to write together our part at the weekend and we were going to talk to Tom and Harry on Skype on Sunday, for the last details, so we could get well prepared for school on Monday.

"To impose itself on crowds, religion had to use strong-arm tactics", granny explained. "Everything different from Christian doctrine was considered as heretic. Many culture books were burnt and millions of innocent people were killed, most of them women. All that with the blessing of seventy Popes at least during three centuries of history. That's shocking, isn't it? Jesus Christ never taught to hate, one of his commandments was instead : "Love other people like yourself". But all that was useful to dominate people, to spread terror, so churchmen became well respected personalities. The idea of sin was instilled: as sinners, men needed the Church's help to be saved, do you understand, terror and dependence, instead of love and sharing as Christ used to preach! Jesus loved Mary Magdalen, in the sense of respect, even if she was a woman and, as they said, a prostitute too. What did his followers do instead? They persecuted, tortured and killed all the people who showed different behaviours or thoughts…"

"But why did they pick on women?", my sister asked her, crouching on her crossed legs and holding a large pillow on the sofa tight, as if she needed protection from something.

"In my opinion, that's because they wanted to take away from them the leading role they used to have. You must remember People turned to them to find support and get advice: their power cast a shadow on priests. In Celtic society, Druids were wise men, they had a never ending knowledge. You certainly remember the character of *Panoramix* in *"Asterix"* stories: he was the druid of the village. For the Celts, women weren't inferior beings. There was a close relationship between men, women and Nature. They worked together with the Divine, they didn't kneel before It to ask for mercy or in search for the eternal Paradise. Their ability to summon natural forces and make change possible was inconceivable for the Church, or we should say that was something they didn't know and, like anything unknown, it scared them. So women scared the Church with their knowledge! The Romans destroyed the oak woods where the Druids used to meet, the Church exterminated witches, who were accused of casting spells, curses, evil magic and bonds, and what's more, of working together with the Devil. Right them, who didn't even know what the Devil was!"

"There's a picture on our history book…" We opened the book, to show her the black and white image of a strange creature with goat horns and hooves.

"Let me see, Sarah…this is *Cernunnos*! The God with big deer horns, the patron of woods and animals. He Doesn't have anything to do with the Devil, maybe just his physical aspect. As I've already told you, people didn't actually know the Devil, that figure was invented by the Church in contrast with God. How could witches worship him and work with him, if they didn't even know he existed?"

"The Church turns bread into Jesus's body, isn't that magic?"

"Excellent, Anne. Catholicism adopted lots of gestures, tools and celebrations which already existed in the pagan religion.

Incense, candles, bells, goblets, water, were all ordinary objects in pre-Christian rituals. I've already shown a part of them, which were later used in Christian religion."

"What are *Sabbat?*", I asked.

"They are the eight celebrations in the Wheel of the Year. We've always celebrated them, since you were children, and I've always called them by their original names."

"Do you mean: Yule, Imbolc, Ostara, Beltane (*May Day*), Litha, Lughnasadh (Lammas), Mabon and Samhain?", Sarah counted them on her fingers like a good school girl.

"Exactly! These are the eight *Sabbat*, which were later replaced by

Christian festivities. You know that Yule is Christmas, when people celebrate Christ's birth instead of *Sol Invictus*. Imbolc is Candlemas, Ostara is Easter (take notice that the words are similar), Samhain is All Saints' Day…"

"But what is true about the Inquisition?"

"Tortured, raped and burnt alive people are true! That's the truth… unfortunately!", granny moralized disgusted.

"What were they accused of?", I went on, as a knowledge-thirsty journalist. Those subjects really interested me.

"There weren't often any charges. A book was even published, the *"Malleus Maleficarum"*, teaching people to recognize witches. Having red hair, for example, a mysterious look, a cat, a strange birthmark, being able to cure fever or to work with herbs like me, was enough…I would have been certainly persecuted and killed, if I had lived four hundred years ago! Luckily, they didn't completely wipe away the ancient knowledge. My grandmother, my mother and lots of women like them were able to pass it on. Just like I'm doing now with you, whether you like it or not, isn't that true, Anne?"

"I'm going to surprise you, granny, but I'm very interested in what you're teaching us, the problem is I'm sometimes doubtful, that's all. Well, I don't believe a candle lit on a certain day, a stone or some incense can change the course of things or influence our life…"

"You're right, a mere candle can't make miracles and that's true for incense and stones too: your mind is the real source of power. It can give shape to ideas and images, give body to your anxiety, fear and beliefs, but also to positive and enthusiastic thoughts. You'll understand from all that the power of prayers, meditation, mantras and visualisations. Your external reality, what you're living, it's the direct consequence of your main thoughts and of the things you believe. Your experiences depend on what you're thinking: if you can change your thoughts, your life will change too! When you have a strong desire which lasts for a long time or is repeated enough in a condition of strong motivation, it can make an evident change happen. Relaxing techniques are used clinically and are taught to reduce the symptoms of a wide range of pathologies. The placebo effect is based on the belief that expectations give rise to a self-healing ability: if someone expects something to happen, it will become true actually. When you want to reach a goal, just imagine you've already reached it! Visualization is very important!"

"What's that?", I got up to light the kettle, but I sat back on the carpet at once to listen with interest to my granny's explanation.

"Visualisation means to see what you wish, just like in a movie. Ten minutes a day with the utmost concentration are enough and, thanks to attraction forces, what you're looking for will come in due time. Do you remember the novel "The secret garden?" You read it some years ago and we also watched the movie together."

"Yes, of course we do. But, what does it have to do with all that?" It was one of Sarah's favourite books.

When a was a little girl, I used to dream of finding a door in the cottage garden, maybe hidden behind the hedge, taking me to a mysterious and unknown place.

"The protagonist of the book", grandmother went on, "I think his name was Colin, says he was making experiments using energy, but he doesn't even know what energy he's talking about, he just knows it's there, he can feel it in Nature. In the novel he uses it to start walking again, in the movie to call back home his father instead. In both versions, the protagonist, his cousin, the gardener and the boy in the heath form a circle, they keep telling some sentences at a hectic pace and they then "throw" the accumulated energy into a fire and into the air. That's just a magic ritual: the energy is summoned, accumulated and finally used to get a goal. It's not so simple, of course, you need both a very strong motivation and the need to make all that come true, for our soul's evolution. We come on the Earth to learn, to evolve. Life after life, we keep learning something more, we improve ourselves. We follow karma's laws. For example, if in this life we strongly wish to be a doctor, but we don't succeed, it's nobody's fault: that isn't obviously the aim of our present incarnation. I just mean that amulets, candles and incense can't solve our problems, they're just means to help us to direct our will towards a goal, supporting us. However, I'm absolutely sure about the fact that, if our will is very strong and we hold on, something will always happen. But I'm straying from the point now…"

"What's black magic?", Sarah asked, still crunching between the sofa cushions.

"Children, magic has no colours. People sometimes use their energy, their thoughts and their will to harm someone else, and that's black magic. There can be different reasons: to get rid of a rival at work, to take revenge after a betrayal…Saying that it's extremely wrong is useless. In my opinion, as I told you about Helen, I prefer pushing negative people away, without harming them.

Of course when I'm wronged, I ask for justice, that's all, I summon Hecate!

However, if your question was making reference to the witches who were persecuted in the past, my answer is no, they didn't practise black magic! They didn't eat children nor joined *Sabba* riding a broom. They were very ordinary women, just like you and me."

Alison came to the cottage too on Friday. As soon as she got off the train, we understood there was something wrong: she wasn't wearing make-up, her eyes were swollen with tears. She kept silent all the way to granny's house, and that was strange from her. I thought of a love disappointment, even if I didn't know she liked any boy.

As soon as she got into the house, granny rushed to her. "Alison dear, what's happened? Come in, I'll make a good cup of tea for you, or do you prefer some hot chocolate?"

"My mum is ill again. Her cancer…it's back in her liver." She started crying, doubling up on herself and falling onto the armchair where my grandmother was sitting just before. Kiki went to sniff her, but she didn't even realize that, shaken with sobs.

"Poor girl! Have you known it lately? How is Stella?"

"Mum is in hospital, they're keeping her there, they are talking about an operation, maybe…"

"Everything will be alright", Granny sat on the armchair arm-rest, rubbing her back.

"What will I do, if she dies, Susan?" Alison had never known her father, her grandparents lived in London, but they were too old to look after her.

"She won't die, darling. By the way, you could always rely on us."

Sarah and I had kept silent, everything was so unreal. We had met Stella some weeks before and she was very well. Wrapped in a long violet cardigan, with a flounced skirt and fantastic ethnical earrings. She showed a glowing smile ad she was proud of Alison's passion for horse riding. Nobody could have thought she was ill again. She had just started working at a wellness centre, where she made Reiki treatments and crystal-therapy: her greatest passions. Everything was at its best…

"I'm sorry girls, I don't feel like preparing the school paper", Alison said, wiping her tears with her hoodie's sleeves.

"Don't think about it", I comforted her without hesitating, "granny helped us to understand some points. Don't worry, it's almost done."

"Thanks. I started collecting material about witchcraft in Italy, in Benevento, last week, but I stopped when I learnt about my mum. Witches probably met there and held their *sabba*. They gathered under a large nut tree and they came flying on a broom: what a foolishness! I read they spread hallucinogenic substances on themselves, so they thought they were flying…"

"Well", granny said, "from what I know about Italian witchcraft, the Benevento nut tree really existed, it was originally a place devoted to Diana's worship. A river called Sabato flows nearby. As far as the ointment is concerned, I wouldn't be surprised if that was really made of substances distorting perception, both then and nowadays. By the way, you can add some folkloristic anecdote to your paper, it looks suitable. But let's stop now, girls. Go to the village and have a walk before dark, you'll be fine. *Cath Kidston* has opened here too, why don't you go and have a look? It's delicious."

That wasn't really my favourite kind of shop, with all those small flowers and dots, Sarah, on the contrary, was fond of it.

She once told me she was looking forward to being eighteen, because she wanted to apply for a job there.

We didn't go to *Cath Kidston* luckily, but we stopped at *Starbucks* to have a *cinnamon shortbread.*

We tried to entertain Alison by talking about boys, horses and concerts, but her eyes were still blurred, as if she was very far from us. We had known her since we were eight, she had no secrets and we had never seen her so worried.

"I'm sorry girls, but I don't feel like talking…I'll call my mum to learn how she is going and to tell her I'm here with you."

She talked on the phone for more than one hour, along our way to granny's house and while we were waiting for dinner. I envied the relationship between Alison and Stella, they were always together. She had told us that she had spent her first years of life in Camden Town, where her mother used to rent a stable to sell her *New Age* products. They spent the whole day there, in all weather, from morning to evening. She played among the dummies and the old vintage furniture in the gothic shop. Everyone knew her and it had been a shock for her to move, but Stella told her they were both free spirits, doomed to travel, and that they couldn't find any obstacle till they were together. She taught her to see always the positive side of things, to be kind to other people and never to judge.

Our mother on the contrary knew nothing about us, about what we thought or what we were interested in. For her, knowing we were the best in our class and buying everything we needed was enough, for all the rest granny was there. We had never been either to the

69

cinema with her, or for a walk in the centre of London or to a picnick. Except for our summer holidays in Palma, we never saw our parents and now that we were growing up, it was still more difficult to meet.

They didn't want us to help them at the cafeteria, we just had to study, they wanted us graduated and fulfilled. We knew mum loved us, but we missed some time spent together in our lives, and with dad still more. Sarah suffered a lot about that, our father was like a super-hero to her, that was probably why she never surrendered to any boy courting her: she wanted to catch dad's attention first, even if that was a very difficult deed, since she hardly ever met him.

"So Alison, tell us, any news about Stella?" Granny had made her fabulous herbs omelette and some pasta with cheddar for dinner, because she knew Alison was crazy for that.

"They're going to operate on her next Monday, they're taking away that part of her liver were the cancer has settled. It looks small at the moment, and just in a certain area. They found it in time because she's always under strict control, less than seven years have passed since the last time. She's staying in hospital for a week and she must follow a strict diet. They say that the liver is an organ which can be regenerated…"

"That's excellent news, Alison!", my granny encouraged her.

"She's tired, she doesn't want to talk about chemotherapy anymore, even if doctors say it's necessary to strengthen the long term effects of the surgery. She feels small…"

"Oh, poor girl! When you hear her next time, please tell her everything is going to be alright and that I'll invite her here for *May Day*: we are going to celebrate the first day of May all together. We are going to hung some colourful ribbons to the oak with our wishes and she is going to explain us the powers of mineral stones. Give her this goal, she will be pleased. We'll have fun, you'll see. It's in two months' time, she will have all the time she needs to recover…"

"Thanks, Susan. She asked me to bring to hospital the box with her stones, I hope they'll let her keep it."

"Don't worry Alison, she will get through all this, your mum is going to overcome this challenge too. I want to give her one of my citrine quartz. Let me purify it and charge it with energy, it'll be ready on Sunday, so you'll be able to give it to her just before the surgery!"

VII.

May Day at the lake

That was a very cold and rainy spring.

Stella's surgery worked very well, luckily. She had to undergo six chemotherapy cycles, once a month till July. Her parents had insisted on having her and her daughter back in London. They were ready to pay her a rent wherever she preferred: Richmond, Greenwich, Hampstead Heath, so they could live in the green but at the same time be next to them. Stella refused categorically, she was scared the city was too polluted for her weak body and she didn't want to jeopardise her daughter's health too. She actually recognised that Reading's air wasn't very healthy as well, but it seemed she had finally found somewhere to live peacefully in Sonning Common.

She couldn't work helping people anymore, she was the one who needed daily *Reiki* treatments from her colleagues. She said they were fundamental to get purified and find her balance once more.

I didn't understand what she was talking about, when she used words such as *"chakra"* or "energetic alignment". I once heard her even calling a snake's name, I think it was Kundalini, which laid drowsing in the second *chakra:* how was it possible we had a sleeping snake inside us? I tried to ask granny, she was more definite than Wikipedia about these subjects.

She told me that *chakra* are just some places in our body where particular kinds of energy accumulate; according to their position, they are connected to certain organs and they rule specific actions and emotions. If *chakra* aren't in harmony, there is a lack of balance and people can fall ill. *Reiki,* crystal therapy and other kind of alternative medicine work this way, to bring new energy and balance.

"Just imagine you have seven centres or spirals or points along your body. The sacral is the 1st chakra, the one of roots; the genitals are the 2nd, the 3rd is the abdomen (also called solar plexus), the heart area is the 4th, the throat is the 5th, our third eye, that is to say the forehead, is the 6th and the head is the 7th." Granny had explained them shortly that way.

I still held lots of doubts about these unusual theories, even if I could see in Stella an enviable peace of mind and force. She never stopped smiling. Of course, she was scared, Alison told us; she was terrified the illness might come back. She kept saying she didn't want to die when she was just forty. But she tried to react, she was a real warrior! She did yoga every morning. "I can't do difficult positions anymore, not at the moment at least…", she admitted. She just restricted to breathing and doing stretching. She then went to the small Caversham Park Pond lake and she relaxed on a bench under the big oaks. She brought with her our dog Ridge to keep her company and she always said that was a magic place, where certainly fairies lived.

"I feel like I'm eighty, Rebecca!", she told her when she came to fetch our dog, "I walk slowly, then I sit on a bench to stare at ducks…but that place is so relaxing."

"That's true. Walking there is very good for you." We all thought the same, it was a nice walk, almost two miles.

"I wish I was still fifteen like our girls. What did you do in Marlow in your teens?"

"It was a nightmare!", our mum burst out laughing, "in the eighties in Marlow there wasn't much to do, to tell the truth. I spent my afternoons at different sport clubs, or at my friend Lucy's, listening to pop music and dreaming of a life in London.

I met Tom when I was eighteen, we got married at twenty and I got immediately pregnant with my twins, so we moved to Newbury and here we are: a life behind a counter! But what about you? What did you do in the coolest capital in Europe when you were a teen?"

"I was a hateful spoilt girl playing the rebel…"

"Were you?"

"I was, Rebecca…You know, money weren't missing, I had everything I wanted: a house in Mayfair, private schools, piano and dance lessons…"

"Wow, Mayfair! Sorry but I can't think of you in the most exclusive neighbourhood in town."

"Neither could I. It wasn't absolutely in harmony with my being, but I soon discovered the alternative side the city could offer. I went out with floating off people, artists and some other shady characters. We went to Soho, Camden and I sometimes walked as far as Elephant, Castle or Brixton. Can you think of that?"

"I heard they are dangerous places."

"Oh, Rebecca, don't play the country girl! They're just lively and multicultural neighbourhoods. Of course, they weren't the ideal place for a blond girl accustomed to having an easy life, but I never had any troubles, I was lucky. I just met lots of people who helped me to understand how varied the word was and who opened my eyes. I had a lot of fun, there were wonderful shops and pubs…"

"Your parents must have been really vexed by your behaviour."

"Of course they were! You don't know how many times they punished me, they stopped giving me my pocket money and they threatened to send me to a girls college lost in the Sottish countryside. When I was eighteen at last, I went to India and I stayed there four years. I almost visited it all, following intensive Yoga and meditation courses. A new world opened for me: my world. When I came back, I was a perfect *hippie*", she said and burst out laughing, "my father was shocked, I was his only daughter, his heir, I hadn't graduated and I was dressed in rags, as he used to say. However, when I was far away, I missed London so much: I love that city, it's life!"

"But you don't want to go back and live there now…"

"I don't, but it's such a sacrifice. I was tempted when my parents offered to pay our rent, but I can understand that's not the ideal place for my health, it's better here, under my oaks and with you, you're my second family now! Just promise me something, Rebecca…"

"Tell me…"

"If I should leave you…will you look after my daughter? She's so young and I've already charged her of so many responsibilities…", Stella started crying and mum hold her in one of her awkward hugs.

"Don't even think about it! Sorry but, where are you going? You're staying here with us and with Alison! I've got an idea: you know my mother has invited us at her house for the *bank holiday* on 1st May, *May Day* as she calls it…As it could be too tiring for you, what do you think if we organise a pic-nick here near the lake where you usually go? It would be nice, don't you think so?"

"Rebecca, I don't know how to thank you. It would be great! But isn't your mother going to work at the stand for the village festival?"

"That's the following weekend, don't worry. What's more, I must admit I feel a bit guilty: we've never had a pic-nick with Anne and Sarah. We've always been so busy with work, so we've lost lots of moments of life together. I didn't worry because they weren't missing anything and my mother has always been a perfect granny, luckily. But parents are very important and we've been neglecting them…"

"It's never too late, Rebecca. You can still put it right. They are two really clever girls."

"Anne is very withdrawn, she's grumpy. I'm worried about what she's like. Sarah is incredibly absent-minded, she has always been since she was a child, I hoped she would get better when she grew up, instead…"

"Anne is just very unsecure, she hides behind her *gothic-dark* look, it's her way to protect herself. She's actually very serious and thoughtful. She still doesn't know exactly how to handle her personality and she wants to be different from her sister, that's usual with twins. Sarah on the contrary is very sensitive and naïve. Without Anne's or your support, she would be completely lost. You should let her be more independent…"

"That's incredible, you know my daughters better than me. Oh, my God! What kind of mother am I?"

"I've already told you, Rebecca. You can still put it right! Why don't

you go to Glastonbury with them next summer? That would be funny. We know you don't like that place, but after all it's a part of your roots and the girls would be really happy."
"But I can't leave the cafeteria!"
"Of course you can. Tom can get through it alone for a few days. There aren't many people in town in August."
"But we're already going to Palma…"
"Come on, Rebecca, that's not the same, you know it too. What can you learn lying in the sun all day and drinking cocktails? I'm ready to bet the girls spend their time there with an I-Pad in their ears, reading gossip magazines and nothing more…"
"More or less…these are our holidays."
"I think it's your absolute right! My parents are going to offer Alison and me a cruise in the Mediterranean this year, we're really looking forward to it. I really need it and I sometimes miss super- luxury!" Her crystal laughter had still the power of giving happiness to the people surrounding her.
"So, are you warning me to go there with them? To that odd village…"
"Yes, absolutely, go…trust me!", Stella encouraged her, slapping her lightly on her shoulder.
"But I've got nothing to do with magic. The fact that my mother is teaching those things to the girls doesn't bother me, on the contrary, I'm pleased they get to know different sides of life. She's making up for what she couldn't do with me, I'm just saying I would feel unwanted."
"You're their mum, you'll never be unwanted."
"Ok, you've persuaded me. I'm going…provided they aren't asking me to climb on the *Tor*, I could never do it", she said puffing dramatically. "Ok dear Stella, thank you for this conversation. Unfortunately I must go back to work. So, it's fixed for the 1st of May, are we all coming here?"
"With pleasure. I'll take you to my magic place!"

We met at Alison and Stella's for *May Day* with mum, dad, granny and Mal. We brought a large packet meal with us, a very happy Ridge, some pliable chairs and some blankets to lay on the grass.

"Stella, dear, you're radiant today! Have you seen what a sunny day we are having? It's all for us!", granny hold her tight handing her a packet.

"Thanks, Susan. It's for me?"

"Open it. It's my latest creation: novelty 2011 for my stall!"

"Thank you, I'm really curious to see what it is, but please, come in now and sit down. My house is small, but the sofa isn't missing. I put some beers in the fridge for the adults and some fruit juice for the girls, please help yourselves. If you prefer, we can go to the back garden."

"When Sarah was a little girl, she told me you had a fairy house in your garden, have you still got it?", Granny asked her, grabbing her by the arm. She was always so affectionate and open-hearted, everybody loved her.

"It's over there… But I want to open your present before."

She undid the packet and took out a fabulous, pink magic wand.

"A magic wand, that's wonderful Susan!", Stella burst out laughing amused, "I really need to cast spells, especially when I go to hospital, I wish I could make everybody disappear!"

"Do you like it? I make them myself. They are presents and can be used as pieces of furniture, they aren't real magic wands. In my opinion, if you really need a wand, you don't need to buy it, you can find it in Nature. But in all modesty, mine are nice, aren't they? I always put a stone on top of them, possibly an amethyst or a ialine quartz, then I decorate them with some glitter, warm colourful glue and beads."

"It's really beautiful, thank you. Young girls must go crazy for it."

"Not just young girls, you should see how many women are asking for it."

We were all sitting in the garden, it was a wonderful day, we couldn't ask for more. Mum and Sarah were wearing flowered dresses, I instead had put a pair of black leggings on and a t-shirt of the same colour with a velvet collar Alison had given me at Christmas. Granny was wearing a long purple dress, Alison a pair of jeans and a blue top and her mother a wonderful green flounced dress with a head band of the same colour. She was very beautiful, even with no hair. She often matched the head band with her clothes, crowning her look with some ethnical accessories. The men instead were wearing shorts and t-shirts as usual. I was feeling alright with my family. We were different, but I felt at peace when we were together, Alison and Stella included.

Mum had been more present than before in our lives for a pair of months. She spent a lot of time talking with us in the evening, she insisted on going shopping at the *Oracle* and she told us she was glad to come to Glastonbury with us.

"This is real magic! You see, all my candles have been useful", granny claimed laughing, when we told her about that.

"Granny, what are magic wands used for?", my sister asked, sipping her apple juice.

"Sarah, don't be boring once more today", I warned her. She couldn't focus all her arguments on the same subject, what's more, when granny started, stopping her was impossible. We never talked about horses.

"Anne, you know how it works. If you don't want to listen to me, then you don't have to. When your sister makes me a question, I think it's right to answer. Well, Sarah, the **Wand** is an invocation means for the Deity and it's also useful to direct energy. When you were children, we watched together *"Harry* Potter" and I told you that you can't do magic just by shaking a wand and telling a magic spell. You need your will and concentration. Let's say we need a wand to direct our will towards a certain goal. People make a circle in some rituals, that is to say a place where energy can concentrate. The limits of this space can be sketched out by making its perimeter with the wand. It can be made with any kind of wood, on my part I prefer the oak, but the most common are made of elder, willow or hazel tree. People say it's the wand which choses its owner. Once you've found it, you should leave an offer to Nature, for example some tobacco or milk, or simply some crumbs of bread. It must then be left under the full Moon light and you can even give it a name! It's going to be your new travel companion."

"Thanks, Susan, I've never had one." Stella was holding her wand in her hand enthusiastically. "So I should think of giving it a name."

"Will you make one for me too, granny?"

I knew my sister would ask for one.

"Of course Sarah, but as I've already told you, mine are just ornamental. You have to find your wand by yourself, it's going to call you. You can go for a nice walk to the park with Ridge and look for it. I'm sure you'll understand by yourself which is the one for you, better if it's not a stick found on the ground. You have to get in touch with the tree, understand if you're allowed to take a piece of it and then thank it. Just if you do like that, your wand will be in harmony with you.

"I keep an acorn in my pocket when I do competitions…" I didn't know why I was telling them.

"Really, Anne?", asked my grandmother turning astonished to me.

"Yes, I found it once when I was riding Nightmare." Nightmare was the horse I usually rode, it was a wonderful specimen of Friesland, "It stopped to sniff something but I couldn't understand what it was sniffing, so I dismounted and I saw it was just an acorn. I automatically took it and put it into my pocket. I've always brought it with me since that day."

"It has turned into an amulet for you, a sort of talisman. It's something you found by chance, but which is precious for you, since you've charged it with energy."

"I haven't charged anything at all!", I said hurriedly.

"So your horse might have done that", granny said smiling. "By the way, by keeping it always with you, you must have transmitted your energy into it."

"Sorry to interrupt you, my ladies", Mal began in his usual gallant way, "how are we going to do for the pic-nick? Stella, are you coming by car with me?"

"Thanks, Mal, with pleasure. I'm a bit tired today to walk over there".

Stella, granny and Mal got into the car, while mum, dad, Sarah, Alison, Ridge of course and I went on foot.

We soon found ourselves in a spellbound place, with a small lake in the middle peopled by ducks and swans, surrounded by very ancient oaks and hawthorn bushes. The small houses nearby were very peaceful and well-kept to the smallest detail, according to the best English tradition. As soon as we got there, a couple of cats moved away when they saw Ridge running in their direction and a squirrel climbed on a higher branch, waiting patiently for the remains of our meal.

"Stella, this place is simply wonderful." Granny's eyes were bright with astonishment.

"I knew you'd love it, Susan. Can you feel the energy? It gives peace, solemnity. When I'm here, I feel I'm a part of a plan, a project bigger than us. Past, present and future seem almost to concentrate in just one moment. I'm happy I can share this day with you. Since I fell ill, I've been appreciating small things better and I'm grateful for every moment life gives me." Stella was really enthusiastic, she was quite moved.

"Coming here is good for you. These oaks can speak to the heart of the ones who can listen to them." Granny was looking around herself, as if she had got to Wonderland.

"Here are your sandwiches", mum called us once more, "vegetarian for Stella and my mother, ham and cheddar for the girls and Mal, and finally a Cesar's salad for Tom and me. Beers aren't missing, there's also water, fruit juice, crisps and some bread for the ducks. Ah, I forgot, I also made an apple pie." She hadn't forgotten even the smallest detail. Even if that was our first family pic-nick, it was great.

Granny had also brought some colourful ribbons to hung. "They're for your wishes, you can put them wherever you want to!"

I chose the dark violet one, as there wasn't any dark. I made the wish to go on living happy moments like that, with the people I loved.

VIII.
Avalon

School ended, we had a six weeks' summer holiday waiting for us before facing our last year at secondary school, then we were going to attend college and, two years later, university. I had left my idea of becoming a vet, I wanted to study "Marketing and Communication" in London instead. I had very definite ideas: I was going to follow the graphic course because I wanted to try to work in the advertisement field later. I liked drawing and I had got fond of Japanese manga recently.

Sarah on the contrary hadn't decided yet, she was living day by day as usual.

Alison on her part was talking about going abroad, but she was held back by her mother's health condition.

By the way, university was still three years far and our only thought at that moment was going on holiday to the Balearic islands and then to Glastonbury.

Our parents let us go out alone at night in Magaluf, probably because they didn't know the small neighbourhood's night life, or to push us to become more open-minded! It was a favourite place for lots of English eighteen and twenty years old who devoted themselves almost exclusively to drinking, from the afternoon till late at night. That wasn't exactly our favourite way of life. Young people of our age had been smoking and drinking since they were eleven-twelve, our class mates had already had their first sexual affairs and we were considered as the "spinster twins."

I wasn't really interested in getting drunk, still less in smoking or having sex just to be like other girls! Our holiday's week finished very fast, we said goodbye to our more and more cheerful and suntanned grandparents and we went back to our beloved and dull England.

We got to Somerset on a rainy August afternoon, after a two hours' trip from Marlow. Mal's rickety Vauxhall Corsa was really too small for the five of us; I spent all the time watching outside, while mum was having a nap and Sarah was singing each single song broadcasted on the radio. Granny was unusually quiet, maybe she was deeply moved because she was going back to her birth place after so many years, while Mal was just focusing on driving, singing with Sarah every now and then.

I loved looking at the landscape, I was fond of the English countryside. We passed by Stonehenge, where my sister wanted to take some photos; we had been given a smartphone for our fifteen birthday and it had become by then as an extension of our hands. Sarah put every single photo she took on Facebook, especially selfies showing her in her dolly looks: pink nail polish, small flowers and her long loose hair, with her dreaming pussycat air. She was like that, the forbidden dream of all the boys in our school.

We passed through small villages made of a few cottages, a pub and the post office, we drove along streets surrounded by a thick vegetation and we finally got to the smooth hills which were our destination. The rain and those grey, low clouds made the landscape particularly charming

"Look, here is the Tor!", granny exclaimed.

At the end of the valley, on the right, we could see that small hill with a tower standing out at the top.

"It really looks like the "apples island" under these low clouds."

"Granny, Avalon doesn't exist", I pinpointed.

"That's true, there isn't any town with that name, but the "apples island" is real and it's just before us. Welcome to the Land of your ancestors, a legendary and magic place…"

We stayed at a nice B&B run by a man speaking in a strange accent and passing himself off as the last Druid in town; he told us his name was Merlin. Granny and Mal burst out laughing in his face, while mum, Sarah and I turned our eyes uneasy. In spite of that strange introduction, the rooms were well-kept, with matching curtains and bedcovers, the porridge tasted as good as the one we used to eat when we were children, and the house smelled lavender. Mal and our granny were in two different single rooms (they still persisted in their platonic relationship!), while we were all three together.

"I wonder how your dad is getting on by himself", our mum thought aloud, dropping her bag on the floor.

"He'll manage to, mum, we're staying here just for four days!", Sarah tried to calm her down. On my part, I was certainly more worried for Ridge than for daddy, it had never been such a long time alone.

The next day the sky was blue again; we were going to visit **Chalice Well** at last. Before we got in, I just knew it was a very well-kept garden and that the symbol of that place were two superimposed circles crossed by a spear.

After we had passed by the ticket office, where a peaceful middle-aged woman worked, we found ourselves surrounded by silence: it almost made us uneasy, but I soon got used to it. We could hear only the water springing and the small birds twittering cheerfully like the characters of a cartoon.

It was certainly a particular and out of time place and in spite of tourists and nosy parkers coming and going, it had succeeded in keeping the signs of a mysterious past. Even there I felt carried away to another world, as it happened when I was at my granny's. The legend concerning that place is connected both to king Arthur and to Joseph of Arimathea.

It says that's the place where the chalice of the Last Supper containing Jesus's blood was buried, the Holy Grail and that the source has been bleeding since then.

Water was the prevailing element.

The first basin was in the form of two intertwined circles, the same symbol which could be found everywhere and that our granny called *Vesica Piscis*. It represented the union between Heaven and Hearth, spirit and matter, reminding mankind that we are a part of the Whole, of two superimposed worlds. Moving further, we found a large stone basin where people could bathe. The water was drinkable, pure and unpolluted, even if its coulour was red. I had read that was because of the high iron content.

The famous well, called "The source", was surrounded by oaks, yews and thorny trees, all of them with a rich history as well: it was the symbol of the continuity between Life and Nature; a passage from the spiritual to the material world.

We sat down, almost uneasy and absolutely silent, staring in admiration at its lid made of oak wood and surmounted by the *Vesica Piscis* made of wrought iron, decorated with vine leaves.

I felt I was a part of something bigger than me, just like Stella had said on *May* Day, when we got to " her" small lake.

No doubts that was a very special place and, for the first time in my life, I could feel pins and needles in my hands: was that the energy granny had been talking about? A thrill went down my back.

"It's powerful, isn't it, my child?", granny was staring at me with her big green eyes. I had already been there with her…I could feel it. I didn't know when or how, but I had already been to that place! She took my hand and her smile made me understand that she was perfectly reading my mind once again. I felt bewildered for the rest of the afternoon. I was at home in that place, my roots were there.

We walked through the cheerful village and we visited almost all the esoteric shops.

"It was completely different thirty years ago", our grandmother told us, "the *Wicca* religion wasn't so widespread, they didn't sell all these articles! I could hardly find colourful candles!"

There was a friendly and cheerful atmosphere, smiling and relaxed people.

"I have to buy a lot of incense, then we'll be free for the rest of the day. I'm going to introduce an old friend of mine to you tomorrow and to show you the house where your mother was born. Can you remember it, Rebecca?"

"Not really, that's why I'm looking forward to seeing it again."

"Don't you want to get on the *Tor*?", Mal challenged them.

"Maybe the girls are going up there. I'm not. I'm not trained enough", mum cut it short.

So the next morning, while granny was visiting her childhood friend, Sarah and I went to the Tor hill. It wasn't very steep, the path was well-kept, there was a slight terracing, so we got easily to the top. We had a wonderful view from up there: fields stretching for a long way and some small village far away. The clouds were still very low on our heads, emphasizing the deep perspective of the sky.

"Wow, it's great from up there!" My sister had already taken out her mobile, ready to take a selfie. "Come here Anne, we'll take a photo together."

She was always very fond of me even if I made fun of her and I often replied rudely. I couldn't make her angry, she was too good, just like granny. I envied them: they were always smiling, they were light-hearted, I didn't understand how they could.

"It's really good, I'll send mum!"

"And then you are going to publish it and tag me as usual."

"No, I'm going to retouch it first, I'm a bit pale…" I rolled my eyes: she was hopeless.

We went down the hill fast and we walked to the town centre, where we were due for lunch.

"Well, did you like it?", our mum asked us.

"It was wonderful, you should have come too! It wasn't tiring."

"Maybe for you…but I prefer looking at it from down here."

"I've got some presents from Grace, my old friend, girls", granny started. "Look how nice they are, they're two pendants: a Pentacle and the *Vesica Piscis.*"

"They're nice, thanks! She's been really kind", Sarah squeaked enthusiastically. "I like the Pentacle. Is it all right for you to take the other, Anne?"

"By the way, you've already chosen!", I grumbled, even if that would have been my own choice.

"We can swap them sometimes, if you want to."

"No, Sarah, they're personal things", granny interrupted us.

"But we are twins!"

"I know, and I also know you're just telling so because you're good-hearted, but once you wear them, these pendants will become one with your energy. They aren't just mere pendants. Do you remember when I told you about amulets? Well, if you wear them steadily, they'll become real amulets, do you understand? There are deep meanings hidden behind a star or some circles. They're symbols!"

"I've often seen the Pentacle here, but I don't know its meaning actually. I like it and that's all", my sister acknowledged.

"It's a five pointed star inside a circle. Each point represents an element: Water, Air, Earth, Fire and Spirit; all of them perfectly balanced. It's a protection symbol; just like the *Vesica Piscis*, the Pentacle stands for creation as well. The "macrocosm" is represented by the circle, while the elements are the "microcosm"; we are all together and connected to the Source, that means the Divine. If you put it upside down instead, it gets a negative meaning, that is to say the rule of matter over spirit."

Sarah has been wearing it since then and she never took it off, not even on her wedding day many years later.

IX

Stella's mineral stones

My sister started going out with Bob during our last year at secondary school; the most beautiful couple in the school was born then: she was the eternally courted girl and he was the boy the county girls desired the most.

Sarah wasn't just one with her mobile anymore, but with her boyfriend too now. They spent all the time at school holding each other's hand, lost in each other's eyes. They kissed whenever they could and that made me feel sick. As if that wasn't enough, Alison found a boyfriend too that year. She met Alan at a Halloween party organized in a deconsecrated church, when she dressed up as a gothic Lolita, and that was love at first sight.

I got terribly bored at that party: my sister was in a corner with Bob, Alison in another one with her latest conquest, most people were drunk and I kept wandering aimlessly.

"Anne, could you be a lesbian?", my sister asked me one day, while she was putting on a lot of mascara in front of the mirror.

"No, I'm not!", I answered angry, "I don't like women."

"Nor boys, actually. Let's go, you can tell me, I'm your sister. There's nothing wrong."

"I'm not a lesbian and that's all. Stop talking crap, Sarah!", I almost pushed her away. It would have been fun to make her make-up smear.

"Don't you like any boy? Neither Liam?"

"Liam has got a girlfriend, you know…" My instructor had found a partner of his same age and I had almost stopped going horse riding for that reason.

"And what about Dylan?"

"Who's he? Mal's nephew?"

Dylan was the son of Mal's younger sister, he was twenty, he studied at Reading university, he had asked my parents if he could lend a hand at the cafeteria to earn some money and he had proved a precious assistant. I had to admit he was a good-looking boy, always kind and with lots of interests, but I didn't believe he could be interested in me.

"I think he likes you, if you only wore something more provoking…"

"Sarah, stop it! We've met only twice and I don't want to change my look just to please a boy."

"You aren't bringing out your qualities, you seem to be trying to hide behind those clothes." That was true. "If you like black, then go on using it, it suits you, but try something more tight, your body is beautiful, you should make a show of it more often."

"Ok, thanks, whenever I need a personal stylist, I'll know where to find her. Now go and meet your Bob."

"Bob is wonderful, we really love each other, you know…and making love with him…Oh-my-God! You can't understand."

"Please shut up, I don't want to learn all details."

"We'll get married as soon as we finish university!"

"Cool! So you've got nine years to organise the ceremony!"

"You'll be my bridesmaid as well as Alison."

"And does the groom know all of that?"

"Of course he does! He asked me."

"Ok, so you can sometimes remind him of that, he shouldn't forget it in the next years!"

During the first weekend in December we were invited to a course about **mineral stones** held by Stella at the *Heart&Namasté* centre in Caversham, where she had been working for a couple of months. She had finished her chemo cycles: they had been very hard but useful. It seemed the cancer hadn't appeared in any other part of her body, but she was still kept under strict control.

She hadn't stopped her holistic studies, she considered them fundamental for the improvement of the spirit and, as a consequence, of the body. She told us she had fun when she had to do with rich posh ladies, they reminded her of her mother. She knew how to deal with them, she spoiled them, giving them at the same time the possibility to find themselves once more through meditation and by watching reality from a different point of view. She had found her mission: she had become a *guru* in Reading.

There were more or less twenty people listening to her, almost all women. The ladies were well-groomed to the smallest details: perfect make-up, just manicured nails, they were suntanned and smiling.

They welcomed us with a non-alcoholic ginger cocktail, one of them dared to ask for a Bellini, but the others told her that staying sober was better, to concentrate more deeply.

We sat on a soft carpet in a nice room with lavender walls, there was a sweet smell of sandalwood incense and a relaxing music in the background, taking our minds to far away countries.

Alison brought her boyfriend with her, he was a quiet guy, three years older than us, he studied architecture and dreamt of visiting Italy. Bob didn't come, that was the first Saturday afternoon my sister wasn't spending with him since they got together.

"He knows I want to become a witch", my sister started talking when I remarked their first separation. "He says I've cast a spell on him since he loves me so much, but he doesn't have to do all the things I do."

"I wonder if you will be able to face distance when you are summoned to *Hogwarts* school of witchcraft and magic!"

"I think I'm too old for *Hogwarts* now", she answered after she had thought about it for a while.

"I was just making fun of you. I'll tell you a secret, but don't tell anybody: *Hogwarts* doesn't exist!"

"By the way, we're going to make up for wasted time tomorrow. His parents won't be at home…", she told me naughtily.

"Of course you're going to study for the text on Tuesday at

school…"
"Not really, we're thinking about something else…"
"If you start taking bad notes at school, mum and dad will lock you at home, you know it, don't you?"
Stella came in at that moment: she was wearing one of her long green dresses, her hair was growing, even if it was still short, she had put a nice make-up and some pendants. She was very beautiful. She greeted us one by one with her hug and her overwhelming smile.
"Please, sit down. Thank you for coming here today. We're going to spend the whole afternoon together, I'm so happy! I'm going to lead you to the fantastic mineral world. This is not a crystal-therapy course, I would need much more time for that. I simply wish to show you these fantastic stones, so you will be able to find some precious allies for your everyday life in them. Each of them has its own particular characteristics…what do I mean with characteristic? I mean both on a physical level, according to their composition, and on an energetic level. These stones vibrate, they have a soul, a very ancient soul. They've been here for millions years, I believe they've absorbed lots of things in this crazy world! Their wisdom can be handed down to us, thanks to all they have gone through, They come from the Earth, they are closely connected to this element. The Earth gives us shelter, it teaches us and gives us all its fruits, we must respect them.
Let's start talking about *chakra*: I suppose you all know what they are…they're the energetic centres in our bodies. The first one, of roots, is associated to red and black; the second one, of sex, mainly to red; the third one, at the solar plexus, to yellow and orange; the fourth chakra, the one of the heart, is associated to pink and green; the fifth one, next to the throat, is connected to green as well and blue; the sixth, our third eye, is associated with violet and indigo; the seventh one, whose name is the crown, to violet, white, and it's sometimes represented as transparent." She put her hands on the corresponding places while she was talking.
As soon as she had finished, she gave everybody a sheet of paper

where a human shape had been drawn and the corresponding chakra centres were shown. She then laid softly twenty stones more or less before herself.

"I'm going to start from the dark stones. Let me make some preliminary remarks: first of all, having all of them is not necessary. I know that at the start, when you've just entered into this world, you can be caught by the fever of buying as much as you can, because you don't want to be unprepared. You're going to realize with time that you're going to work actually always with the same stones, according to what you're like, to your aura and to your needs. Let's make an example: a dear friend of mine persuaded me to buy a wonderful Malachite, she described and praised it so much; so I decided to buy it, I kept it next to me for two months, I tried to understand it and to work in synergy with it. No use, it wasn't the one for me! We didn't get on well together. On the other side, I'm working hard with the Tiger eye at the moment, a stone people don't always like."

"What have you done of your Malachite?", asked a woman with long eyelashes and fluorescent nail polish.

"I gave it back to Nature and left it under a tree. Some goblin might have taken it of course…" This sentence made many people smile and giggle, but we all knew Stella really believed in the "Little People", she often said she saw fairies and we respected her for that too.

"I'll warn you to buy them just in specialized shops. You should avoid the Net just because it would be better if you kept them in your hand and got in touch with them, before buying them." As she talked like that, she kept turning in her hands a light pink spherical stone.

"You should purify them, as soon as you get them. Just imagine how many hands must have touched them."

"What do you mean by purify?", my sister asked.

"How is it possible, a future witch who doesn't know what purify means?", I made fun of her quietly.

"That means wash them, Sarah. You can put them under a jet of spring water or even in your sink, leave them under moon rays, lay them on a piece of amethyst or simply run some incense over them…you know, I prefer dried up and burnt sage. I think the best thing is always following you instinct. But let's go on now, if you have any question, you can ask me in the end. Here's **Black Tourmaline**", she said, lifting a delicious black spherical stone. "First and second *chakra,* it's a powerful protection stone. It's very useful to protect us from electromagnetic fields generated by computers, electrical devices, mobile phones and so on. Everybody should keep one, especially in the office. Wonderful Tourmaline pyramids are sold, they can also be used as pieces of furniture. What's more, it helps to feel deeply rooted. In my opinion, you shouldn't wear it as a pendant, since it's connected to the first *chakra*: it would make you heavier, it's better if you hold it in your hand, next to your sacrum, knee or feet. It must be often purified. Remember that black can protect and wipe negativity away, so it helps to overcome insecurity, stress and neurosis. Let's go on with **Hematite**. It's associated with the first and the second *chakra* as well. It looks sprayed with metallic paint, doesn't it? It's wonderful in my opinion, and it's the ideal stone for people who can't find their place in the world, their roots. You can't imagine how long I have worked with this stone when I wandered aimlessly. She brought me here in the end, I could never thank it enough. On a physical point of view, it soothes any kind of pain: headache, period pains, stomachache, intestinal and kidney pain. They're useful to give you a strong positive charge. The ideal position is to keep them under your heels during meditation. I often work also with another stone, **Heliotrope**, for the second *chakra*. It brings peace, it strengthens our immune system and it's a good luck talisman, because it protects us from unwished external influences. I use it a lot at the first symptoms of cold or cough. A very famous stone is **Obsidian,** which is still associated with the first and second *chakra*: it gives protection, peace and wellness. Its main quality is the ability to reflect our defaults: it makes us see the sides of ourselves which we usually want to hide, it makes the truth come to light. It should be used during meditation   only   by   well-trained   people,   while   it's perfect as an amulet for everybody.

I will go on with these two **Jaspers.** There are many kinds of Jasper, mine are red Jasper and breccia Jasper. The red one is connected to the second and third *chakra*, you can use it for blood problems; it teaches us that the Earth is our mother, giving us everything we need. The breccia Jasper is very powerful instead, it helps us to get on our feet once more after any kind of defeat. When I was told that cancer had come back again in my liver less than a year ago, a felt I was a victim, a defeated woman. But then I understood I had to turn into a warrior, I had to go down to the battle field once more: I didn't know how all that would end, but I had to go on fighting. In order to face the situation with my head hold high, I relied on my breccia Jasper, besides my own will. When the doctors were talking to me during each check, I held this stone tight in my hand and I could feel a powerful force inside myself. It protected me, it wiped away negative energy and pessimism."

"How is that possible?", a young blonde woman, probably in her forties, interrupted her. "Don't misunderstand me, Stella, I'm not saying you're not telling the truth, I only wonder how a stone could do all that."

Those were my own thoughts more or less. Our granny used stones too, but I've always mistrusted them because I didn't understand their potency.

"Ok, I'm going to interrupt my descriptions for a while, to try to answer you. First of all, stones are just tools. Some people work with colours, other ones with sounds or just with *Reiki,* you can do yoga or relax reading books, you can find your inspiration by drawing or get free of your anxiety by running. In my opinion, the most important thing is feeling well with yourselves and, to do that, you need to find the tool which better harmonizes with you. You could probably hold one of these stones in your hand and don't feel absolutely nothing; there's nothing wrong in that! As I've told you, they've got a soul, they're alive. They can't speak, but they can pass their very ancient knowledge on by the way. I can feel their power.

That's not just my prerogative or the one of some chosen people. Once you get the basic pieces of information, the ones I'm showing you today, you should devote some time to listening to the stones, if you want to understand what they are telling us or what we are expecting from them. Just choose a stone, the one which inspires you the most, keep it with you for one or two months, and then draw your conclusions. You can't understand, if you don't try."

"Isn't that just suggestion?", I started saying. "Sorry Stella, I'll explain it better: we've been told that a certain stone can protect us or give us strength, so we obviously get persuaded about that, but that's just our mind persuading us, it's just a mineral after all!"

"Well said, Anne! That's why I'm telling you to try. You shouldn't believe everything you are told. As I was telling you before, for my friend Malachite is a super-powerful stone she can't do without; it was just the contrary for me! You should try."

We all kept silent and nodded.

"Well, my friends, I don't know if you're too, but I'm thirsty. Let's have a break."

"Could I possibly have a Bellini now? Or just a beer?", the same woman as before asked.

We all burst out laughing.

We all got back to our places after ten minutes and Stella started talking again.

"So, what was I saying? Oh, yes, let's talk about **Carnelian** now, very useful for the second, third and sixth *chakra:* it gives us an ability of socialization and pragmatism. It gives balance to our emotions and improves the functions of small intestine. It overcomes the fear of death and lets us have access to the memories of our past lives. It protects us and makes us enjoy the moment. I gave one to a friend of mine some years ago: she got pregnant after a while, it was an unexpected pregnancy, but her life became better after that; she had a very beautiful daughter. She asked me if my stone had hit her, and I answered that wasn't possible at all, that stone had simply made a necessary change easier, which had come in the shape of a baby. She had been asked to live her moment and make a choice. Another fantastic stone is **Amber**. It acts on the fourth and fifth *chakra*. It's a resin actually, not really a stone. I used it for my daughter during her teething: a nice amber necklace and we could dream peacefully. That's true Alison dear, isn't it? Now my little girl is almost sixteen…Amber soaks up pain and strengthens our immune defences. It transmits positive energy and wipes away depression, if you just look at it. This is **Citrine Quartz** instead", she said showing us the stone my granny had given her. "I didn't know it till my dear friend Susan, who is also Anne's and Sarah's grandmother, gave it to me. Its yellow colour and its connection with the third *chakra*, that is to say the solar plexus area, makes us understand why it's a support for all the organs situated in that area of our body: liver, spleen, stomach, bladder and pancreas. It's a very important area, I call it a "passage area". Both our positive and negative emotions are revised here. Just think about being in love: people say they feel butterflies in their stomach; when they're angry instead, their stomach is closed. Everything passes through the solar plexus. Preserving it is very important. Citrine quartz is a very precious ally to bring peace inside us, optimism and to increase our self-esteem. We have also the **Tiger Eye** for the liver. It interacts with the second and third *chakra*, it's excellent for wealth, money and against negative forces. If we keep it on ourselves, it can help us understand the real nature of the people we meet. We can go up to the fourth *chakra* with **Pink Quartz.** It's the main stone for love and fertility, it brings love towards ourselves and other people; it reduces stress and anxiety. You should always keep it in children's rooms. And now, the first aid stone: **Rhodonite**, fourth *chakra*, so called because it helps to overcome the shock due to accidents. It brings peace, it wipes mental confusion away, it reduces stress and it finally arouses forgiveness. We should learn to forgive ourselves, to accept our mistakes and to understand that making mistakes is something human. Rhodonite helps us accept our faults without being overwhelmed by them. If we go on, we'll find **Aventurine:** it interacts with the first, fourth and sixth *chakra*; it brings joy, happiness and enthusiasm. It can especially help us dream and make our dreams come true, it makes us understand what are the right things for us. When I was working in Camden, I sold a lot of good luck amulets made of aventurine; they were the favourite ones to bring wealth and propitiate money gain. I held one of them on the counter, strangely nobody ever stole it. Look, here is **Amazonite**, it's useful for the second, fourth and sixth *chakra*: it works on overcoming bad habits, it releases you from blocks and helps you not to feel a victim, but the master of your life instead. It delivers you from tiredness, even the one due to the liver, and it's rich in potassium; it's very helpful after a weakening illness, because it balances the vital energies in our blood. It was a powerful helper for me, it's absolutely my favourite together with amethyst.

I've recently been given a **Sodalite**, fifth *chakra,* that's called the thyroid stone too. People often mistake it for the lapis lazuli, but it's different because it doesn't have streaks. It helps us make decisions and be understood when we aren't. It soothes troubles coming from emotions, for example stress, anxiety and anger. It helps our respiratory system to work well. One of my favourite is also **Labradorite**, this stone is useful for the fifth and sixth *chakra*. It can produce plenty of ideas and helps us find the truth. It leads us to appreciate our abilities and hidden qualities. If you wear it as a pendant on your neck, it's a protection and what's more, it increases the charm of the people wearing it.

Here we come to the **Moon Stone,** which usually interacts with the second, third and fourth *chakra*. It's white, slightly opaque, it has a soothing effect, it protects us from our own emotions and it mitigates moody attitudes. It's connected to femininity, it's helpful during our period to reduce the pain, and during menopause as well. It can also stimulate media abilities and clairvoyance. I always keep it next to me when I'm not satisfied about the way I look like; it helped me a lot during chemotherapy, when I was losing my hair and I couldn't face these changes. I kept it in my pocket for the whole period and I slowly started to smile again…I can say that is a precious support which helps us face important renewals in our life.

Is there anyone who doesn't know **Turquoise**? It's in connection with the fourth and fifth *chakra*, it's used as an amulet, it brings good luck and it wipes away negativity and evil eyes. It's also excellent in case of anorexia and as a generic tonic, it helps us tell the truth.

If there are students among you, I'll warn you to take **Fluorite** for the sixth *chakra*. It helps to get the highest levels of creativity and increases our mental focus; it's also used to develop our intellectual abilities and to make our thought faster. It's the ideal for astral trips and to heal family ties. It soothes skin, bones, teeth and mucosa's troubles.

And here is my best friend! **Amethyst,** sixth *chakra*. The stone par excellence, without belittling the others. A protective mother for the people wearing it, it purifies by taking up negative energy and turning it into positive qualities; it'll reassure you if you keep it in your hand and it'll help you to overcome addictions. People once thought, in fact, that it could help to stay sober. Cardinals' rings always had one amethyst mounted in them, as a sign of absolute power, because people knowing the spirit can also dominate matter. What's more, its violet colour gives out a special vibration which is able to make our sixth sense stronger. For that reason, it's associated with the sixth *chakra,* our third eye, which is the home of our intuition. I've got an amethyst druse on my night table, it's not big, more or less 10 centimeters, and I usually put on it the other stones to purify them because, as I was telling you, it takes up negativity. The last one, but not at all the less important, is **Hyaline Quartz,** which influences the seventh *chakra* and is a sort of bridge between spirit and matter. It has been considered a magic stone since ever, because it wipes away both physical and mental troubles. Just think that the famous crystal spheres, with their hypnotic and divinatory qualities, were made of this stone! It brings balance to our cerebral functions and it pushes away stress, it finally supports us on our way on the Earth.

Well, with this last stone our presentation comes to the end. Thanks everybody for listening to me. I think we'll have another break now, then I'm going to explain the last things. Have you understood everything till now?"

Some people approached Stella to make her questions. She was evidently tired but satisfied, she had completely caught our attention and had written down on the paper the most important information about each stone.

"Oh, Alison, you mother has been really great! Everything was very clear", my sister told her stretching her legs. "Would you like to come to granny's next weekend? I'm going to introduce Bob to her. Come with Alan as well!"

"With pleasure. Would you like to, darling? So we can have a tour in Marlow! Susan is really a fantastic woman." Alison was always very sugary when she was talking to Alan, as if he was the most important man in the world…and he probably was for her actually: she had never known her father, she needed a male presence.

I should find some excuse to avoid going, I couldn't stand being with all those lovers kissing all the time and whispering love words to their ears. They got on my nerves! I was really looking forward to going to university in London, I had to stand just two more years at college and then I would be on my own at last.

"I haven't told you how you should use the stones", Stella said after a ten minutes' break. " I'll advise you to meditate, or even just to relax, while you keep the stone next to the involved part of your body. I've already told you that each mineral stone is related to one or more *chakra* and that these ones are connected to certain parts of our body. So, for example, if I want to improve my hepatic functions, I'll put my wonderful citrine Quartz next to my solar plexus area or, still better, on my liver. I should keep it there from ten to fifteen minutes."

"What if I don't have time for meditation and relax?"

"I really can't meditate at all and when I go to bed at night, I immediately fall soundly asleep", two cheerful middle- aged ladies interrupted her.

"If you really don't have time, you can keep them in your pocket… still better if you hold them in touch with your skin, fixing them with some medical tape, the one made of paper, I mean. Jewels can be finally a solution: bracelets, necklaces, pendants, earrings…"

"And what about men?", asked a red-hair, very kind boy, smiling.

"You can keep them on your desk, in your wallet or in your pillowcase. If you like them, there are pendants and bracelets for men too."

"Stella, is your pendant a white Labradorite?", Sarah asked her. She had always loved it since she was a child; she could still remember its name.

"You almost got it! It's not a Labradorite, it's an **Opalite**, sixth and seventh *chakra*. Mine is not artificial, it's completely natural. I was given it when I was almost of your same age. It can strengthen your emotional balance, so it's useful at times of change; it besides calms down aggressiveness and widens psychic abilities."

"It's wonderful!"

"It really is. Thanks, Sarah."

"So, besides purifying them and keeping them near us", she went on, " charging your stones is very important. What do I mean? You should pass them on your wishes, the reasons why you're using them. As I've told you lots of times before, these stones have a soul, they vibrate, you should get in touch with them. Chose a stone to work with, keep it in your hand, you can speak aloud or, if you can't, you should just focus your mind on your final goal. Tell it openly what you're expecting from it. It might look strange, but you are going to feel much more connected with your small friend after that and it will give you a powerful energy!"

I thought that looked really strange, by the way I was going to try.

"Where can we buy stones, Stella?", I asked her.

"There are specialized shops, or you can find them at fairs. I don't know about Reading, but I can give you some names of the shops in London."

"We could buy nice Christmas presents for ourselves", Mrs. *I*-want -a- Bellini started.

"Great idea! After that: once the stone will have finished its work, you can clean it, thank it and let it rest for a while."

"What if we break them?", I wanted to know.

"If you break them, Anne, it means that their work is at the end; you can give them back to nature."

After she had finished her explanation, we all got up and thanked Stella.

She had been really great.

"And now, if you wish, you can go on talking at the pub at the end of the street. On my part, I'm going back home, I'm very tired."

"Are you OK, mum?", Alison asked her.

"Yes, I am, darling, don't worry. I just need to get some sleep!"

"Are you sure? Alan and I are coming with you..."

Sarah and I went home too, mum came to fetch us, she wanted to know about all the things we had learnt.

I was less skeptical about stones, I was certainly going to buy one in the future and try to put my trust in it.

X
And here he came...

I let the cheerful couples visit my grandmother the next weekend and I asked my parents if they needed my help at the cafeteria.

"That's really great news, Anne!", our father commenced. "We have really hard work at Christmas time. People pour in floods into the *Oracle* for their shopping, and when they got out, they feel like having a nice cup of hot chocolate or tea. We never have rest! Dylan is excellent, but we'll be very pleased to have some more help, if you come too!"

"Is Dylan going to be there too?", I asked. I hadn't considered at all the fact he was going to be there too; I got blocked every time I met him, I didn't know why. It was probably because he was always trying to get in eye contact with me, and that made me incredibly uneasy, or because he was older than me or simply because he was so damn sexy.

"Dylan is always there, he's great", mum told me, "he really helps us a lot. He's really Mal's nephew, he's kind, smiling and helpful. You can't imagine how many girls get inside just to have a look at him!"

I could imagine, actually.

I arrived at the cafeteria at eight in the morning to help them clean and prepare all the things needed for such a long day. I had never been behind the counter, I had no idea at all about how to make coffee or anything else, I couldn't even use the till, the only suitable work for me was cleaning the tables and sweeping the floor.

"Hi, Anne! How are you?", Dylan asked me kindly as soon as I got in. That wasn't difficult to answer.

"I'm fine, thanks." I should maybe ask him how he was, or how was university going, but I didn't.

"Is Ridge OK?"

"My dog?"

"Yes…"

I was so silly, I didn't know any other Ridge, he was obviously referring to my dog!

"It's fine too…"

"Great!"

That was the end of our first short conversation.

I spent the whole morning clearing and cleaning tables. I couldn't believe how many people where there, they were always coming and going. Smiling and hurried people came in, dragging behind them bulky bags full of presents and letting the typical icy winter air come through the door.

I was already worn out at lunch time.

"Have a break. Half an hour", mum told us.

What was I going to do for half an hour? I wanted to sit down, I couldn't feel my legs anymore, but I didn't know where to go. I couldn't stay in the back room alone with him…

"Go Anne, go and sit in the back room, have a sandwich if you like. It's evident you aren't used to working!", my dad made fun of me.

I didn't have a sandwich, my stomach was closed, I just took my mobile. I sat in a corner staring at the phone screen. Dylan was sitting in front of me, he was watching his smartphone too. Well, he was probably writing his girlfriend…My heart was hammering in my chest. What was happening to me? I didn't was to raise my eyes. I felt suddenly examined; he was looking at me from above his mobile. Damn it! I kept our eyes contact, I didn't want to show weak.

"What's up?", I asked him.

"I was trying to understand if you look like your grandmother."

"No, I don't", I cut it short.

"But you're quite like her instead…"

"I'm not! She has got red hair, mine are dark. Her eyes are green and mine nut-brown…"

"My uncle has always been secretly in love with her…she's a very beautiful woman indeed! I've never understood why they don't live together."

"Neither have I…they could be a nice couple actually!"

"They probably like it the way it is."

"Of course…"

He was still staring at me, right into my eyes. He wasn't intrusive, he seemed to be looking for something in me.

"Stop staring at me!", I couldn't stand it anymore.

"It's difficult not to stare at you. Sorry…"

"Why do you find it difficult?", I asked intrigued.

"Because you're a mystery!"

"What do you mean?"

"It seems you're hiding something…"

 Boys used to tell my sister the same things, to conquer her. We had obviously something in common.

" I can never understand what you're thinking about with your deep eyes…"

"I'm not hiding anything at all! I have no reason why", I burst out.

"I know. But you're really special, in spite of that! Your sister is special too, I must admit it, but she has more malicious ways. You're more intriguing. That's it, I've found the right adjective: you're intriguing!"

I couldn't understand if that was a compliment or something else.

"Are you coming here again tomorrow?"

"Yes, I am. Is that a problem?"

"You can come every day for me. So I could be able to get to know you better, by staying next to you…"

I spent the afternoon just like the morning, much more people came and it seemed that closing time was never coming, even if it was dark outside.

I caught Dylan staring at me again; I stared at him too, he moved skillfully behind the counter, he was always smiling and he understood in advance all the customers' needs. He was surely a precious member of the staff for my parents.

Sunday morning was much more peaceful.

"People are sleeping", my father told me.

"Or they're hanging over", Dylan said.

"Did you go out yesterday evening, my dear?", my mum asked him.

"Yes, I could never say no to a beer on Saturday night, but I was already in bed at eleven o'clock. What about you, Anne? What did you do yesterday evening?", he asked me.

I had gone to bed at nine, like a good child.

"Anne?", my father said, "they don't go out at night yet. The cinema or a dinner with friends at the most. They have their curfew at eleven. Sarah is making us crazy this year! She hasn't been studying since she found a boyfriend; I don't know how she's going to pass her college entrance examination. We should start to punish her."

"And Anne, have you got a boyfriend too?", he was still staring at me, as if I was the only person in the room.

"No...", I answered, staring back at him defiantly.

"She has never had one", my mum confessed.

"Never?! Such a beautiful girl!"

He went on with our game of glances all day long. I liked challenges, I wasn't going to surrender neither to his flatteries nor to his charm

We found ourselves together in the back room once more, there was an unbelievable energy between us, which was growing like a magnet as moments passed by.

"Do you like being a *dark*?"

"I'm not a *dark*, I just like black..."

"Are you always answering as an asshole?", he asked me smiling.

"Yes, I am…"

"Why?"

"Because I'm just like that", that wasn't difficult to understand.

"You're hiding…"

"Sorry?", I didn't understand.

"You're hiding behind this bully attitude, this black nail polish…But your eyes can't tell lies. I'm not saying you're insecure, on the contrary you absolutely aren't! You simply don't want to be noticed. Don't you think other people can match you up?"

"What are you studying? Psychology?"

"No! Economy…", he burst out laughing. "Can I have your number?"

"Sorry?"

"I don't know when we will meet again…"

"At Christmas!"

"Will you give me your number at Christmas?"

"No, we're going to meet again at Christmas. My granny always organizes Christmas Eve's dinner at home. Come with us. Or do you celebrate only Yule?"

"How do you know I celebrate Yule?", he asked me astonished.

"You're Mal nephew, I think you have his same beliefs, there's absolutely nothing wrong about it! We've grown up following the Celtic calendar too, but Christmas is Christmas, so we have dinner on the 24th, to make things easier."

"I celebrate both days as well. I will be pleased to come, thank you."

"By the way…here you are." I wrote down my phone number on a piece of paper fast and I tried to slip away, but his arm was blocking my only way to escape. He was keeping staring at me.

"You like when I'm looking at you, don't you?"

Of course, I really liked it, but I couldn't confess it.

"I don't mind…", I lied.

"That's not true!"

"So, what do you want me to tell you?"

"That you're giving me time…"

"Time for what?"

"To get to know you…", he told me in a whisper.

I was going to give him all the time he needed.

"If time is what you need…I'm not in a hurry", I answered whispering too. He was still blocking my way and staring at me, so I passed past him squeezing up against the wall and brushing my breast against his chest deliberately, till I saw him start. I addressed to him a malicious smile and he finally turned his eyes without stopping smiling.

I got a message few evenings later.

Dylan: Hi! What are you doing?

I stopped breathing, his photo on *Whats.App* showed him in the foreground, he was really nice. I checked mine: it was a manga character. Maybe that was a bit too childish, I thought. I was going to change it.

"Who is it?", asked Sarah lifting her eyes from her book. She had been punished as expected. Her last school test had been really bad, she couldn't go out with Bob after school in the week anymore and our parents had limited her use of her mobile, or at least they had tried to; when they weren't at home, she still used it actually.

"So, who is it?", she insisted.

"That's not your business!", I answered.

"Oh, come on, you're blushing. I always tell you everything about me."

"But I don't ask you, it's you who want to talk about it! By the way, it's just Dylan."

"Have you given him your number?"

"Yes, I have, I can't see anything wrong in it. I've also invited him at granny's at Christmas Eve."

"Wow! So you really like him. Bob won't be here for the holidays unluckily, he's going skiing to Switzerland with his family."

"Poor guy…I really couldn't have chosen between a cottage in

Marlow and a chalet in Crans-Montana.”
“Granny has really liked Bob and Alan.”
“You’ve told me thousands of times, Sarah!”
“Her opinion is very important to me”, she went on, “but, you know, she doesn’t want to help me with school.”
“What do you mean?”
“I asked her if she could charge some stones or light some candles for me, you know, the things she usually does. She answered I just have to study; if we need some more help for my college entrance examination, to increase my concentration or get a goal, she will be happy to help us, but she isn’t going to do anything for me at the moment. I was a bit disappointed.”
“Your test was so bad because you’ve lost your mind since you met Bob, you’re always thinking about him! Granny’s magic would be wasted, a candle or some incense can’t replace your study, do you understand that?”
“That’s true, I’m always thinking about him, but I can’t avoid it, we love each other so much!”
“Don’t start talking about getting married”, I immediately interrupted her.
“So tell me, what did you answer?”, she suddenly changed the subject.
“To whom?”
“To Dylan.”
I hadn’t answered him yet, but that looked easy. He was asking me what I was doing, I answered lapidary.
I: Studying
Dylan: What?
I: Maths.
Dylan: I can help you with your homework, if you want. That’s my favourite subject! *Emoji* with glasses and a book.
I: Thanks, but I can do it. If I need your help, I’ll ask you.
Dylan: Ok, see you at Christmas. I’m really looking forward to!
I simply answered OK and I immediately changed my profile photo. I found one of me in Palma de Maiorca.

Dylan: That's not fair, you're gorgeous!
I: Just remember this, I'm not in a hurry…I prodded him.
Dylan: Neither am I…now! But I'm not going to become like my uncle and your granny, I won't be still courting you when I'm seventy! He added some smiling emoticon.
I didn't answer. Maybe I should give myself some time to go out with him, but I was scared by the fact he was already at university, he was four years older than me, and then I was going to London after college, I wasn't probably going to see him again.

It was by then a tradition for Stella and Alison to spend Christmas Eve with us at granny's. Alan wasn't there, he had gone back to Liverpool to visit his family.
"I haven't seen Bob for three days", my sister sighed, flopping on the sofa. Old Kiki just got up to go and sniff at her and to get her caresses, then it went back to sleep on its cushion.
I was wearing a short, black, close-fitting dress with opaque stockings and my *Dr Martens*. I had chosen that dress because Dylan was going to be there, of course.
"You're so nice! What a pity for your shoes…", Sarah had judged.
"I'm not wearing high heels!", I cut it short.
"Have you noticed, girls? I've used a lot of mistletoe this year", our granny exclaimed.
"Unfortunately our boyfriends aren't here", Alison pointed out laughing.
"You're right, my dear! I hadn't thought about it."
"Kissing under the mistletoe would be so nice…", Sarah sighed.
"Mal gave me a lot and I wanted to use it all for my decorations. Take it as a love and union sign, even if your boyfriends aren't here. I wish you to be always happy, girls!", granny went on while she was laying the table.
"Mistletoe doesn't have any roots, does it, Susan?", Stella asked her, sitting down next to Kiki's cushion and caressing its small black

head.

"**Mistletoe** was a sacred plant for the Celts just because it didn't have any roots touching the ground, so they believed it to be a very pure plant", granny explained. " people say their seed is left on certain trees, like oaks, by some birds which are messengers of the Gods, that's why it represents the union between the spiritual world and the Earth. Its berries are white, they remind us of sperm, for that reason it's considered as a symbol of fertility. They say it brings love, fertility, health but also protection; people thought indeed that hanging it in houses or haylofts kept fire and lightning away!"

"I've heard someone say that they used to put it in babies' cradles to prevent fairies from stealing them and replacing them with an elf." That was Dylan's voice, I hadn't realized he was already there and he was just behind me.

"Hi, Dylan! Let me look at you, you're getting more and more good-looking and tall. We never see you here in Marlow", my granny told him hugging him fondly.

"I just come here for the holidays."

"Are Rebecca and Tom making you work hard at the cafeteria?"

"No, they aren't. I really like my job", he answered. Our eyes crossed at that moment.

Granny followed his gaze and her face was crossed by a malicious flash, then she addressed a broad smile to me.

"Oh, no…no...no!", I thought. "I don't need granny to plot anything to make me closer to him!"

"That's not fair", he whispered in my ear while he kept standing behind me.

"What is not fair?", I asked him turning and staring into his eyes. My legs were trembling slightly, he was really handsome with his roll neck blue pullover and jeans.

"When you dress up like that, it's not fair", he claimed without turning his eyes from mine.

"It's Christmas", I told him nonchalantly.

"You're so beautiful!"

"Thanks."

Alison, Sarah and Stella started staring at us too at that moment, as if they were watching a movie: some pop-corns were just missing! They couldn't hear what we were saying, but the electrical charge in our gazes was clear, anyone could notice it.

"Ok, girls", Stella interrupted them, "let's go to the kitchen and help Susan."

"Oh, I don't think granny needs it", my sister said naively.

Alison elbowed her aside. "Let's go, Sarah", she ordered, dragging her away to leave us alone.

We kept staring at each other.

"There are two things preventing me from making a move on you."

"What makes you believe I'm going to agree?", I asked him lowering my face.

"I'm blocked by the fact that I work for your father and that he's actually in the room next to this at the moment."

He hadn't answered my question, he was clearly sure I felt his same attraction. Well, it wasn't like that.

"The second problem is that you're just fifteen. Damn it, you look eighteen…look at your body!"

"Is age a problem for you?"

"You're underage! I could get into trouble, do you understand that?"

Mal came in at that moment to put some logs next to the fireplace.

"It's freezing outside, guys!"

"So, Dylan, are you staying here in Marlow for the holidays?", I tried to find a neutral subject because of his uncle's presence.

"No, I'm just staying for two days. I'm going back to Reading on the 27th. What about you?"

Mal went out. We were alone with Kiki and the lit fireplace.

"You would get into trouble only if I wanted to", I told him, getting closer without losing my eye contact. I wasn't going to put him into trouble.

"You're driving me crazy, Anne! I can't understand you, you're always exciting me, but you're keeping your distance! We're clearly attracted to each other. Or I am at least. I'm always thinking about you!"

I felt the same, but I couldn't admit it.

"I want to take it easy. I'm just going to send you messages, till you finish school at least."

Granny came in at that moment with some Christmas candles Stella had given her as a present.

"Have you seen how beautiful they are? They smell cinnamon! Ehi, wait a minute: look where you are, my children, raise your eyes!"

There was a mistletoe composition over our heads, hanging from the chandelier. It was really nice.

"Do you know what that means?"

Dylan lowered his eyes and I started laughing uneasy.

"You should kiss. Come on, it brings good luck! I'll let you alone", she winked at me and was gone. Was that one of her magic tricks? I hadn't noticed that mistletoe before.

"I clearly can't take it easy. It's a conspirancy, the women in your family want to cast a spell on us. First your granny with my uncle, then you with me…What's your secret, apart from being so beautiful?"

"Do you think that would bring bad luck, if we don't kiss under the mistletoe?"

"I don't want to risk!"

"There's my father in the next room, he could come in anytime…", I couldn't finish talking: he had come closer, staring at my lips and keeping his hand softly on my back, near my pants. He then looked at me as if he was waiting for me to agree. He pushed me gently against him and he put his mouth on mine. It was soft, it was moving slowly. My head started turning. He started nibbling my lips, he was coming closer and closer. He was damn sweet. I didn't know what to do, I took his face into my hands and we kept staring at each other with our usual passion. His kiss became deeper and deeper, I couldn't stop. I liked being so close and so in touch with him. Before it was too late, we parted panting. It all lasted just for a short time, but we couldn't risk.

"You're not running away from me, miss! This is just the beginning", he whispered before he joined the others at table.

"Just remember: I'm not in a hurry", I answered, fixing my dress on its sides.

My sister and Alison dragged me to the bathroom as soon as they could, and wanted to know all details. I just told them we had kissed under the mistletoe.

"On your cheeks?", Sarah ventured.

"No", I answered in a dull voice.

"So you are getting together now?"

"No", I went on.

"But he likes you!"

"We're giving things time."

"Why", Alison asked astonished.

"Because he's almost five years older than me!"

"Alan is at university too! That's not a problem for us, on the contrary…"

"And then he works for our dad."

They still couldn't understand.

"Yes, but he's Mal's nephew. We all know he's a fantastic guy! Anne, you've been lucky…you know, all the girls are crazy for him, but he has chosen you!" My sister was really happy; the fact that he was so courted by the girls made me feel terribly anxious.

We never went out at night, I knew nothing about university students' night life. No…it couldn't work between us.

It was granny's turn later. As soon as she found me alone in the kitchen, looking for the *Worcester* sauce, she asked me, "Have you kissed under the mistletoe?", without any roundabout words.

"Yes", I answered shyly.

"Excellent, it will bring you good luck! But tell me, do you like Dylan?"

"Yes, I do."

"He really likes you."

"He told me, but I have trouble in considering us together. He's too old!"

"How do you feel when you're close to him?"

"Attracted!"

"Just that? Let's put apart physical attraction. Of course, it's important and I understand that it's very strong at your age, but I'm asking you how do you feel as a woman. Do you feel at ease, at peace? How do you feel inside, I mean."

"I feel as if he was a part of me, my extension. I feel at ease, it's difficult to explain. I feel OK next to him, but I don't know him. Come on, granny, he's five years older than me. It can't work!"

"Who knows? Just give things time. If you feel so well when you're close to him, that's because you were doomed to meet. Your souls are connected."

"How can he waste his time with me? I still have to finish school, then I'm going to college and then to university in London."

"He's going to London too!"

"When?" Dylan was going to London too? I didn't know that!

"I know he wants to finish his studies there. He's applying for a scholarship. I don't know when he'll go there, in a year's time I presume. That's fantastic, isn't it, my dear? You'll meet there. So you'll also have some support."

"I think that's it."

"But don't think about it now. Try to get to know each other peacefully. I always say that: give things time."

XI

Blue Bell's Wood

Spring came as fast as lightning. Dylan and I only exchanged messages. I fell asleep every night with his "good night" and I woke up the next day with his "good morning".

I often went to the cafeteria to see him. Dylan was very fond of pets and, all the times I took Ridge with me, I felt moved when I saw them playing together. He was really good with animals.

Our relationship was moving further, even if very slowly. I knew I had to think about school first and I couldn't get distracted. But he was just going to stay there, next to me, waiting for me in spite of that.

The worst time was the weekend, because I didn't know where he went nor what he did at night. I knew he went out, but not where and who he went with. I wore myself out by imagining him in certain places till late at night, maybe drunk and with girls hovering around him. I hadn't added him to my contacts on Facebook for that reason. I preferred not to know.

He asked me to go out in May.

Dylan: You birthday will be on 25th, won't it? *Emoji* with cake and candles.

I: Yes…How do you know?

Dylan: Your granny told me (*emoji* with hearts in the eyes). I'd like to take you to a magic place to celebrate, you're going to see blue-bells and we could have a pick-nick (heart).

I knew there was a birch wood full of blue-bells near Reading, but I had never been there. They bloomed from May till June. Was he referring to that wood? My mobile lightened again.

Dylan: Darling, look at the waxing Moon now and I'll do the same. Our eyes will meet there!

I: How do you know it's waxing?

Dylan: I really have to teach you everything. It's waxing. Its crescent is on the right…look at it! *Emoji* with moon and heart.

I moved to my bedroom window, while Sarah was following me with her gaze, feeling curious.

"What are you doing?", she asked me.

"I'm looking at the moon."

"Oh, you're so romantic! Since when?"

"I just wanted to check something."

There it was, more beautiful than ever. A smiling slice of light in the darkness of the night. I could see all the stars. There wasn't any cloud.

I thought Dylan was doing the same thing: he was looking at the moon too…I felt at peace and protected. He was there for me.

Dylan: Are you looking at it?

I: Yes, I am, right now.

Dylan: So am I. Good night my child. *Emoji* with heart.

I gave up study for an afternoon and he took a day break from the cafeteria, so we could go to Nuffield Place Wood.

He had no car, we caught two buses and we walked for a long way through the fields, but we got there at last. The landscape was wonderful. Very tall birches surrounded by a blue carpet. It looked like a picture.

We found a small place were to lay our plaid. I had brought some sandwiches and he had brought some drinks.

"What did you do yesterday evening?", I couldn't stop me, damn it.

"Nothing special yesterday, I just went to the town centre. And you?

Did you celebrate your sixteenth birthday?"
"I had dinner at a Spanish restaurant with some friends of mine, it was nice."
"Are you ready for your exam?"
"I think I am."
There was a moment of silence, when Dylan took my hands and came closer, staring right into my eyes.
"I'm moving to London in September. I got my scholarship." He stopped, then he went on. "I'm sorry to tell it just today, but I had to do it."
"Congratulations! You're really great." I was really happy for him.
"Thanks." He wasn't at ease. Maybe he had thought I was going to be dejected or something like that.
"How long are you staying in London?", I asked him.
"I don't know yet, but I think I'm going to stay there. Will you come and visit me? It's not far from here. I don't want to lose you, Anne", he was holding my hands still tighter. "But I don't want to ruin your life or live a distant relation."
"Do you know which university course I'd like to attend, Dylan?"
"You told me marketing and communication."
"That's it, two more years at college and then I'm going to university in London. And to tell the truth, I had already chosen it before I met you. So, the distance would only be temporary. Of course I'm coming to visit you, and you're coming back at weekends, aren't you?"
"Are you really just sixteen or twenty? You're talking like a girl much older than your age."
His smile was overwhelming. His eyes were shining bright and he couldn't stop staring at me. We had been waiting for this since Christmas, for a moment when we could be closer and alone.
It was all so unreal: the trees, those delicious blue-bells, the little birds twittering. We were alone in that paradise. He and I. Nobody else. We kissed again and it was wonderful. We felt more relaxed

here, we didn't have to bother about my father rushing suddenly into the room. I was thinking about nothing except him and the fact we were close. We couldn't part. His hand found its way under my t-shirt. He was staring at me and smiling maliciously. He was touching my breast and I started. He was so sweet, everything was so perfect. We both wanted something more, but that wasn't possible. Not there, not at that moment.

I bend my back against him, to feel his presence better.

He was the first to move away.

"It's so difficult, Anne. You're perfect, damn it! I want you."

I was staring at him confused, I had never felt anything so deep.

"Ah, I was forgetting", he tried to recover his composure. "I've got a present for you." He took a packet out of his backpack.

"For me? Thanks!", I hadn't expected it. The most wonderful thing was being there with him.

I unwrapped the nice violet paper. It was a book. My hands slipped on the title in relief: "The Moon and its magic." I raised my eyes from the cover to his face, with a puzzled look. Dylan was smiling. "Since you don't know anything about Moon phases, it looked perfect for you."

I felt charmed when I learnt that waxing Moon had very strong and special energetic qualities, how they could influence us, how they changed according to the month and time of the year. "Getting in harmony with its phases is very important", I thought inside me.

"Are you interest too in this kind of "things", like my granny?"

"I don't know exactly about your granny, apart from her oils, tinctures and things like that..."

"She's always talking about energy, especially mind energy", I told him turning the pages over. "I never feel anything", I confessed. I knew I could tell him everything. "I never feel the energy in the world around me. I don't feel anything about stones, I can't read cards, I let even mint die!"

He started laughing amused.

"Come on, everybody knows mint is a weed and it grows easily. But with me, it lives a very short life. Even Kiki always ignores me! And I've never believed that lighting candles or incense can change our life."

"That's true, lighting candles and incense can't change anything", he claimed.

"You just need your will and concentration", I went on. "I know. The problem is, I don't even believe in that."

"Have you ever experienced pins and needles in your hands?", he asked me, staring at me as he usually did.

It didn't make me feel uneasy anymore, I liked it. He seemed to be trying to read into my soul, to be really interested in me. I was sure that making love with him would be an overwhelming experience. I tried to wipe away that thought from my mind.

"Yes, I have. I felt pins and needles in my hands just once, before the well in *Chalice Well*!" I started twisting instinctively my *Vesica Piscis* pendant in my hands.

"Did you feel anything special?"

"I had already been there, I belonged to that place. That was the only time and it was a very deep feeling."

"Do you ever feel anything else?", he kept asking me.

"I feel I'm getting into a parallel reality when I go to my granny."

"That's a magic cottage", he claimed. "It has a unique atmosphere which can take you through space and time." He stopped talking for a moment. "We kissed there for the first time", he said hesitating.

He bent on me once again, without turning his eyes. He then held me and put me on himself. We kissed for a while, his hands always under my t-shirt.

I let him do everything he wanted. "I want to be the first boy you will make love with", he whispered softly to me. "Just promise me."

"I couldn't do any other way."

It was just a question of time. We belonged to each other.

"And what about you?", I asked."What kind of energy can you

feel?"

"I can feel an energy in the shape of physical attraction at the moment", he told me smiling.

"I don't mean now. I can feel the same very well! I mean if you have any special aptitude for magic…"

"Of course! I'm going to tell you about it sooner or later. I feel well in touch with Nature and with everything belonging to it: animals, trees. I try to listen to the emotions coming from the world surrounding me. I can feel there's something more beyond the material world."

I was happy for what was growing between us. He was a very deep boy.

We went home late in the afternoon. As we were sitting on the bus on our way back home, our hands never parted. Suddenly Dylan made me look out of the window, showing me the waxing Moon which was already bright in the sky.

"It's the couple's Moon, the Moon of May."

"What do you mean?", I asked him, keeping fiddling with a lock of his hair.

"The God and the Goddess got together at Beltane."

I didn't understand.

"You should read the book I gave you. Every month, with waxing moon, you can study the characteristics of that special moment. Just follow the Moon, it'll show you your true Nature. I'm going to look at it with you, even if we aren't physically together.

XII
The Moon

The following months weren't easy.

We studied hard for our exam and we passed it. Alison and I got an "A", Sarah a "B". She had finally chosen the course she wanted to attend: education science. She wished she could be a teacher at primary school. That was surely the best choice for her, since she was always so patient and sweet. She could handle children very well. That was what she used to say at least. I don't believe she had ever really got in touch with them.

I saw her shattered just once in our life. Sarah was the quiet and balanced one. She never cursed, even when her mobile fell to the ground and the screen was broken, or when she threw some jam on herself or still worse, when she let nail polish drop on the carpet. These were very ordinary things for her. However, she never got upset. She said at the most: "Oh! What a pity." And she shrugged.

It was a hot afternoon at the start of July when she got to the park, where I was running with Ridge. I saw her come in her white dress and her smeared make-up. Something very serious might have happened. My sister was always perfect.

She texted me, asking me where I was, and I answered. I couldn't have imagined she would turn up soon after in that state!

Ridge jumped on her, cheerful as it always was, soiling her completely. Strange, but she didn't seem to care about that.

"What the hell has happened to you?" I had never seen her like that before. I showed her a bench we could sit on.

I couldn't calm her down, she kept crying, holding her head in her hands.

"Sarah, what happened?" I caught her by her shoulders, shaking her. Ridge kept sniffing her, trying to catch her attention by his pawn or putting its large muzzle under her arms. It had perfectly understood that its young owner had serious troubles.

"Bob…" she said, looking at me, her mascara streaking down her cheeks together with her tears and her pink eye shadow.

"What did he do to you?" I had already understood, but I wanted her to tell me.

" He left me!"

" What a bastard! So suddenly, you met and then he left you, did he?" I knew she had spent that afternoon with him.

"Yes. I met him in the town centre. When he saw me, he didn't kiss me, he was far away." She kept sobbing.

"I asked him what the problem was, but he took me to one side so we could talk. His family is moving to Woodley and he doesn't feel up to go on with our relationship."

"Woodley? Bullshit, it's just on the other side of the town! Dylan is moving to London and he doesn't have any trouble", I burst out. I was beside myself with anger.

"That's what I told him! We could meet at the weekend, but he was unyielding", my sister cried. "He doesn't feel for me anymore."

"So he doesn't feel for you all of a sudden, does he? What a worm!" If he had been there at that moment, I would have socked him on his dude face, he was just a spoilt brat and that was all.

"I didn't hear him much lately", she went on fiddling with the hem of her skirt, "I thought that was because we were studying hard. Can you realize it, Anne? That's the end of my life!"

"Don't talk nonsense. You're sixteen, you're gorgeous and he's just a bastard". I really thought it.

"Yes, but I love him."

My sister didn't deserve to suffer like that, she was too good and naïve. Nobody should make her suffer, least of all that cheeky-face-Bob.

Sarah spent the following days crying in our room. She didn't even want to go to granny's. She wandered in the house like a zombie, eating lots of ice cream (I wonder why people with love troubles usually drown their sorrow in ice cream), she didn't put any make-up and she kept her hair tied. I couldn't recognize her.

As if that wasn't enough, Alison came to our house one evening, she was shuttered too. Alan was leaving for his one-year *Erasmus* in Venice. She wasn't crying, she was just very angry.

"He had never told me he had applied for a scholarship!", Alison shouted. "He told me suddenly some nights ago, as if that was the most beautiful and simple thing in the world. He didn't want to worry me, as I was studying to prepare me exam. Do you realize that?"

I tried to justify him, but Alison added to.

"He should have told me! My mum was right when she told me I shouldn't trust him, her cards had said that, but I preferred not to listen to them."

"All men are bastards, Alison!", my sister burst out. She never cursed, but now her sadness was turning into real anger.

She tried to have her revenge in Magaluf, she used all social networks to show herself in very short dresses and high heels, hugging any English boy she found in the street (and that was quite easy) and kissing a different one each evening.

She retouched each photo precisely, to show herself still more suntanned, and she posted it on Facebook at three at night (she set the alarm clock just for that), so Bob could see it, while she was having fun on the Balearic islands. In return he got engaged with Grace, the daughter of some family friends.

I told Sarah of his bad behaviour, but it was all useless.

"I don't care, I'm playing dirty. That bastard must eat his heart out. He made me get three kilos fatter because I was on the pill."

"Were you on the pill?"

"Of course! I didn't want to get pregnant at my age! The only positive side is that my breast got bigger too", she claimed satisfied, wrapped in a pink top.

"But did mum know?"

"Of course, she took me to the gynaecologist."

I ignored everything. I was the virgin sister and I was going to be for a long time, as Dylan was going to move to London.

He organized a leaving party at the cafeteria. My parents were really sorry he was going away. They weren't the only ones.

"Oh, Dylan, we're going to miss you a lot. You've been our best helper ever", mum told him sighing sadly.

"Come and visit us."

"I'll do it! London isn't far. I'll often pass by."

He said that staring at me. I knew he was going to do that, but I was broken hearted by the way.

I didn't want to go the cafeteria to say goodbye that day, just there where everything had started. But he had insisted on it.

He texted me. He needed to see me, so I went.

"Have you started my book?", he asked, handing me a *donuts veg*, my dad's new speciality.

"Not yet. I'm going to start it next January; that makes more sense."

"As you like. Are you coming to see me? You should start to settle in the capital city, if you're going to move there too in two years' time. I'll be waiting for you, you know", he whispered, taking my hand softly without turning his eyes as usual. I was going to miss his eyes.

"I'm coming…I don't know when."

"Come on, Anne, you can come just for a day too. The train leaves you in Paddington, and I'll be there waiting for you."

London had always attracted and scared me at the same time. It was so big; I wasn't used to it, I was surely going to get lost with all that underground lines. But Dylan was right: it was really near. Once I understood how to move, I could go and visit him in a day very easily.

College was very demanding. Sarah, Alison and I were always together once more, with no boys around us. Well, my sister had a lot, but she never got engaged with anyone. We just parted when we didn't have any lesson in common. We lived as one for the rest of the time, like we had since we were children. We often visited granny, who always welcomed us with her broad smile and a good smell of apple pie. Time seemed never to go by for her.

"Sarah, I'm happy you aren't going out with Bob anymore", she confessed. "He was too superficial for you. Now, just enjoy the fact you're almost seventeen and don't take things too seriously. You have all your lives to do it."

She was always very busy in her kitchen, or engaged with her knitting. In spite of her worker bee behaviour, she never missed a thing.

"Anne, what can you tell me about Dylan?"

"He's in London."

"I know. Have you ever met again?"

"No, but we text each other almost every day." I started as soon as I heard my mobile ring. Everything was going well, London was fantastic. He missed me and was waiting for my arrival. He kept sending me photos: of his student house, of *dark* shops, concerts, streets decorated for Christmas. He was only a few kilometers far from me, but he was so far away.

"Why don't you go and see him?", granny asked, while she was throwing crunchy into Kiki's bowl. "Come on, big cat, don't be lazy. Poor Kiki! It's almost blind. Anne, tell me, why don't you go to London?", she went on.

"I'm going in May." We had agreed I was going for *half term*.

I had decided I wasn't going before because I didn't want to see him in his new life. I feared something between us had changed. I was still a sixteen years old immature girl, living in Sonning Common and wandering in parks with her Golden Retriever, nothing more. He was a very good-looking twenty-one years old boy attending university in one of the coolest cities in the world.

I flipped every month through the book Dylan had given me. I couldn't do without anymore.

It started with the **"Wolf Moon"** in January. Wolves wandered in search for food, they moved in packs in that cold winter month. We must remember our roots, pay honours to our families. The wolf is connected with the dog in the first card of Major Arcana: the Madman, that helps us to take the right direction. It represents a time of concentration and reflection. A time where Mother Nature is at rest and regenerates.

Dylan remembered I was going to start the book in January, so he texted me on full Moon day.

Dylan: Look at it. I'll always protect you. You're a part of my pack.

I made fun of him in reply, telling him we were not in *"Twilight"*, among ware-wolves and vampires. The truth was I missed him and I was waiting for full Moon to feel closer to him.

February represents **"Immaculate Moon"** (like snow) and it comes at the same time as Imbolc, that means "into the womb". Everything gets possible: our goals are easier to reach.

However, we first need to throw away all useless things, so we can make our minds clearer. Just as granny taught us with the broom Mal gave her every year at that time.

March is the month of rebirth, of resurrection, of Ostara. Nature wakes up and spring comes. The **"Seed Moon"** remembers us that we must in fact till the garden inside ourselves with our good intentions and with qualities useful to become better. Animals reproduce in April. **The Hare** is the most important symbol of fertility, whose name is associated to the full Moon of this month.

It's a period of deep changes, both inside ourselves and in the world surrounding us.

Dylan: We are going to read together the May Moon. How long are you staying here?

I: I'm arriving in the morning and I'm coming back to Reading in the evening.

Dylan: OK. Better than never! I've already decided where to take you!

I arrived in Paddington on a hot Saturday morning in May as we had arranged, I found Dylan waiting for me there. He was even more good-looking than I could remember. We hadn't met almost for a year.

"Wow! You're gorgeous!"

I was wearing my usual black leggings and a top the same colour. Following my sister's advice, I was wearing the most low-necked. "Your breast is beautiful, show it." So she had convinced me. I didn't feel much at ease, but I surely made an impression on him. We kissed as if that was the most natural thing we could do. We didn't care about being in one of the most crowded train stations in town, surrounded by thousands of hurried people pushing us. We were alone, he and I.

"Oh my God, Anne, I've been missing you so much!"

I couldn't answer. My head was still turning. I was inebriated by his perfume and by that kiss.

"You're going to be seventeen in a few days."

"That's true."

I didn't understand what he meant by those words. Maybe that I was still under age, so we should wait a year more to make love? My sister had been on the pill when she was just fifteen and that was normal, from what I had heard.

"How are you going in London?", I asked him.

"It's fantastic. You'll see, you'll love living here."

"What are your plans for today?"

"I'd like to take you to visit something in King's Cross, then we could go to Hampstead Heath. If you don't prefer doing something else. But please, don't ask me to go to Oxford Street or Piccadilly Circus on Saturday afternoon."
"Don't worry, I'm not interested in those places."
We got to a very crowded King's Cross after standing half an hour on the tube, pressed by a human flood. By the way, I didn't dislike being so close to him.
"What shall we see here?", I asked.
"Doesn't this place remind you of anything?"
"It reminds me of "*Harry* Potter"."
"That's it. Look there."
And there it was, platform 9 ¾ with a trolley driven into the wall. I couldn't believe it.
"Oh my God, Dylan. That's great, thanks." I hugged him enthusiastically.
"Take a photo of me, so I can send my sister. We've dreamt of coming here since we were children."
A satisfied smile spread on his face.
"That's what I adore about you, your naivety!". He kissed me tenderly on my forehead. I felt protected when I was with him.
"How is Ridge?", he asked me, grasping my hand.
"Unluckily, it has developed a dysplasia in its hip."
"Poor big dog. And what about your parents? And the cafeteria?"
"They're muddling through also without you, they miss you, and I'm missing you too."
"We're going to be here together in less than a year. Well, about that, have you already decided where you're going to stay?"
"No idea at the moment." I didn't even know where my university was situated.
"Would you like…well, would you like to rent a room with me?"
I stared at him incredulously.
"Am I rushing too fast?"
He really was.
"Oh my God, I don't know." My voice was trembling.

"Just think about it."

I thought that talking about living together at the age of eighteen was really too early, even if I felt very tempted and it was surely cheaper to share charges. I was going to think about that!

We spent the whole afternoon wandering in Hampstead. The view from up there was great.

"Have you seen? London is fantastic from here. It's my favourite place in town, followed by Hyde Park and the riversides of the Thames."

"Stella used to live here. You know, she suggested me to take new habits when I move here. Giving a name to a place where I can find a shelter if I want to run away from the city mess, choosing a café where I can have breakfast, a pub where to rest at night, that kind of things."

"Stella is right. London is magic, you are never alone here, but you can find yourself again at the same time. There's a great feeling of freedom. It looks as if everything was possible here; I've found my dimension, the place I had been looking for since ever. I just miss you now, to make it still more perfect."

I stared at the city down there, it didn't scare me anymore, even if it was wide.

"I'm sorry, I've forgotten the book about the Moon."

"Don't worry. We're still in the waning Moon phase. What do you think about it?"

"It's interesting, I like it. Let's say it's connected and it completes what I know about the sun phases."

"Of course, because the God and the Goddess are connected, like the Sun and the Moon. May celebrates the **"Couple Moon"**. There's a great turmoil in Nature: everything was born in that period, love stories included", he winked at me. "We celebrate just that at Beltane: the union, the coupling. It's one of the most powerful Moons in the year. All goals, even the most difficult to come true, seem easy to reach."

It was soon time for me to go back home. I felt a bit like Cinderella. That day had gone too fast. I was leaving Dylan to his London life, to his Saturday evening with friend I didn't even know.

Everything was so absurd. I suddenly was really looking forward to moving there, to staying with him every day, sleeping with him and waking up hugging him.

"I'll be waiting for you here again, Anne. As you see, we aren't so far away."

It had been a wonderful May day.

"Thanks, Dylan. Come back too among provincial people like us sometimes", I joked.

"I'll come."

He kissed me and I wished that would never end. My train came and I couldn't stay there. Not yet.

There were record temperatures in June in England. I found sleeping at night very hard. I left the window open, letting Moon rays light my room.

It was "**Honey Moon**", honey as nutrition and as a symbol of the transformation made by bees.

Nature is now in a phase of metamorphosis, like us with her. What was blooming at Beltane becomes a fruit in this period: it's a time of plenty and prosperity.

Sarah asked me if I liked the book I was reading and I answered it was very nice.

"I'm going to miss you. I'll be alone in this room in a year's time." She started crying.

"Please, I'm not going to war. It's just twenty minutes by train. You'll be lucky to have me in London: you'll always have a pretest to come and go shopping. Why don't you and Alison come to university there too? It would be great."

"Alison would never come, you know, Stella wouldn't agree. I'm very well here, I don't feel like living anywhere else. It's all so comfortable here."

She was right, staying there would be much easier. My parents
would spare a lot of money. Bu I felt that wasn't what I wanted. I
had to give Dylan and myself a chance, at least.
"Will you leave here your book about the Moon before you go?"
"Of course. Have you given up your witchcraft studies?"
"I'm reading *fantasy* books and look, I'm going to show you
something secret." She took out a big box, she opened it and handed
me some wonderful drawings of fairies, dragons and castles.
"They're great. Have you done them?"
"Yes", she told me uneasy.
"Wow! That's real surprise! I didn't know you could draw so well,
little sister. You should study graphics, not I. You must publish
them."
"I relax drawing and these images can bring me to a different world.
I think that's my magic."
"You're incredible. Really."

The July Moon brought the end of the school year and it's called
"Herbs Moon". It's connected to the beginning of the spiritual
harvest, after all the changes which took place in the previous
months, and also to the real harvest of the herbs which we need for
our magic works; just like my granny used to do, drying them in her
cottage kitchen.
August is the month of reaping, we have in fact the **"Grain Moon"**:
wheat comes back every year to give us food and energy. It reminds
us that life cycles, death and rebirth, are necessary. Changes always
bring a teaching with them, even if they're dramatic.
I met Dylan again at the beginning of September at last. He came
back to visit his family in Marlow and my granny organized a lunch
at home to welcome him. It was still hot, so we had lunch in the
garden.
"This is the "Indian summer". September is always a wonderful
month", old Mal told us, while he was placing the outdoor bench.

Kiki had left us that summer. A part of our childhood which would never come back again.

Sarah had wept her heart out, then she had decided to bring our granny another kitten at once. We brought it home just that day. It wasn't black, but three-coloured: it looked like a *British*, even if we weren't sure about that. We called it Bell, because it liked the sound of bells.

Dylan was the happiest of us all. He was really very fond of animals and he was very good at dealing with them.

"Why don't you take one in London as well?", granny asked him.

She still wasn't so enthusiastic about having a pet at home, but I knew she was going to get used to it very fast.

"Not now. I'm often outside for my lessons or something else."

I wondered what that something else was. I preferred not asking.

"When I put up with my own family, I'll surely take a pet. I'm really looking forward to!", he said sincerely, looking at me.

I didn't want to be like my mother, who was already married and had two twins when she was just twenty. No, no, no, absolutely not! Living together was ok, but talking about having pets or starting a family looked premature to me.

That was exactly the day of "**Grape Harvest Moon**", it's time to feed the wisdom inside ourselves.

We spent a cheerful day all together. I felt at home and relaxed with the people I loved. Our last year at school was waiting for us, then our big jump.

"Please, Dylan, take care of Anne, when she's in London", my granny told him, knowing how to interpret my thoughts and being surely more fluent in her talks, after she had drunk two glasses of excellent *Rioja*.

"I'll always take care of Anne, don't worry", Dylan answered smiling, holding my hand tight under the table.

I felt a thrill going down my back. I wished I could kiss him there, before all the others. Unfortunately, I just looked down uneasy.

We have the "**Blood Moon**" in October, a symbol of sacrifice: period blood, the blood of the animals we used to kill in the past, when men needed hunting for food (and not just as a useless sport like today), blood like the colour of autumn leaves falling and feeding the ground. It's the Moon devoted to a period of rest.
Just like the one in November: the "**Fogs Moon**".
A period of meditation, wrapped in the darkness of the season, when we thank Nature for the gifts it gave us and also for the future ones. It warns us to believe in the immortality of the soul.
The book ended with the **"Oak Moon"** in December, as a memory of the everlasting fight between King Holly and King Oak, that is to say the alternation between the light and the darkness period. It's time for new promises and for the coming back of the Sun.

XIII
Ogham and not just that...

"I'm going to take a gap year, I'm going to Norway!", Alison said suddenly. Stella was almost going to faint. It was no accident that she decided to tell her mother the news when we were all there. We could support her and make the atmosphere less tense.

"To Norway? For a year?". Nobody knew anything about that. I didn't even know she liked northern countries.

"Mum, you went to India when you were as old as I am now, and you stayed there for four years."

"I did, but India is hot and colourful."

"India is extremely dirty and far away", Alison underlined. "Norway is dark, cold...", Stella kept saying.

"By the way, what are you going to do there?", I asked interested.

"I don't know yet. I think I'll meditate before the fiords view."

She perfectly knew that a few words were enough to keep her mother calm: to breathe, meditate, incense and veg food. When she wanted to go and eat somewhere, her winning card was claiming they had also a veg menu. It was always like that.

She played the ace of meditation that day.

"Everything considered, Alison, the good thing is that you could study Runes when you're there, so we can add them to my course about Ogham."

Stella had deepened her studies on **Ogham** with my granny. They had attended a course in Marlow together and she organized tours in the parks with her rich posh clients from Caversham. It was incredible how she could make these elegant women hug trees and get in connection with them.

133

She told us shortly what it was about and it was really interesting. "Does Dylan know this ancient writing?", I wondered.

The Celts used a group of symbols both as a form of writing and as a calling to the tree world, evoking certain energies coming from them.

Stella explained that the letters were very important and powerful. Those symbols could pass messages and information on, but also make certain events come true or not. With Runes it was the same.

Each symbol was very simple in itself, as it was made of straight lines (which could be easily cut on branches or stones) and it was associated with a tree. The name "Tree Alphabet" came from there. It was undoubtedly used by the Druids for code messages.

I also knew from my grandmother's stories, that ancient people used to divide the year into thirteen months, each of them made up of twenty-eight days, in harmony with moon cycles. A stock day was left, that was the winter solstice's eve, the time of the year when the year dies and which the Celts represented by the yew tree; the following day, when the sun was born again, was associated with the fir in their calendar. The creation of a tree calendar connecting a tree to certain times of the year came from there. I didn't know anything further, I had never heard about those Ogham symbols and even less about their meaning.

Stella began to explain them, starting from **Beth**, the birch, the tree of beginnings.

It's the first one to be covered with leaves again and for that reason it's associated to spring rebirth.

Besides, it's deeply connected to the Moon (because its trunk is white) and to Goddess Brigid, who is celebrated at Imbolc in February, the time when the "light in the womb" brings the promise for a new start. That's why brooms, used for purification, are also made of the wood of this tree.

The second symbol is **Luis**, wild Sorb, famous for its red berries. It stands for the tree of awakening, of coming back to life. The red stands for blood in fact.

The third symbol is **Nion**, the Ash tree. This Ogham, according to Stella, has the same meaning as the "Force" in Major Arcana of Tarots: it's the symbol of the maturity we need to control our instincts and keep our interior balance. That's why it was a sacred tree for the Druids and their sticks were made of this wood, as a symbol of wisdom.

We then have **Fearn,** the Alder. This tree is spiritually compared to humankind's way on the Earth, to a river flowing. It grew especially on isolated islands in the middle of water streams, where people used to build oracle temples; its presence there was considered necessary to use the oracle power in the right way.

Saille, the Willow, is very beautiful and strange. It's connected with Water too, to time passing by and to life and death following each other. It's linked to Goddess Ecate and it's an inspiration symbol for literary men.

"May bush", **Huath** or the Hawthorn couldn't be missing, whose white flowers remind us of chastity and purity, and also of defense, as Mal told us in the past.

Just like granny told me many years before, **Duir**, the oak, is certainly connected to the word *door*. It's considered as a link between the material and the spiritual world. The depths of its roots can be compared to the tallness of its branches, it's like a bridge, a passage between two realities and it pushes us to open the doors of perception.

Tienne, the holly, is the most important protection tree. Just like **Coll**, the hazel, it's a symbol of wisdom. People used to believe that by eating its small fruit they could get the knowledge of all occult arts and sciences. It's also associated to number "nine", the "Hermit" in Major Arcana, that is to say the wise man, the one who made a search inside himself and got a higher level of knowledge.

Things were different for the mistletoe, a seed parasite plant which has no roots and it's considered as a gift from Heaven, so it's sacred. People could only pick it up by a golden axe (which was a typical Druid's tool). That plant is a symbol of rebirth and survival.

Quert, the apple tree, has always been the tree of knowledge, considered as the fruit of our desires and as the tree of learning. A strange event is connected with it: when an apple is cut perpendicularly, its peduncle will reveal a pentacle: a five-pointed star composed by the seeds, that are men and matter surrounded by the spirit.

Muin, the vine, is instead a symbol of harmony, cheerfulness and joy, which are the feelings coming from wine.

Another meaningful plant in Ogham is **Gort**, the ivy, associated to the Goddess and a symbol of females. His spiral growth reminds us a promise of rebirth and resurrection.

Ngetal, the Rush, is in connection with the flow and with the different phases of life, because it grows half in water and half outside, so it's a symbol of two worlds: the material and the spiritual one; it's the tree of introspection, of winter, just like **Ruis,** the Elder, which is associated with darkness, death, with cold and dark moths. It's the tree of witches and magic. It makes us feel the need to go from one phase of our life to another and it gives us the braveness to look straight at our shadows, at the dark sides of our personality.

Idho, the Yew tree, which is often poisonous, is for that reason a symbol of death and it's placed in graveyards. Its resin's smell can cause a consciousness alteration, making shaman journeys between different worlds possible.

Ailm, the Fir, stands for rebirth, or to say it better, being an evergreen, it reminds us that life keeps going on; death is just a passage to another world. It's certainly considered as the symbol of winter solstice, the time when the sun rises again. **Ohn**, the Broom, is compared to the sun at spring equinox, maybe because of its yellow flowers which are so similar to the light coming back at that time of the year.

White **Eadha**, the white Poplar, makes us think about the wisdom of elderly people, of the ones who have already completed their journey of life and learning. It's the tree of eloquence, considered as the ability to communicate at the right time and to keep silent when we just need to listen to.

My granny gave me a small bag containing a plant called **Ura** according to Ogham, the Heather, which stands for good luck and love. She told me to bring it always with me to London. She certainly did it to help my relationship with Dylan. I was sure deep in my heart that she could see in the two of us what she and Mal had never been. I also knew that heather was put into brides' bouquets and it was considered a powerful talisman for good luck.

I couldn't believe how many interconnected things my granny and Stella could show us.

She went on with her explanation, saying it was possible to use small sticks with symbols cut on them, and make divinations. However, she just walked in Nature, found a certain tree and tried to get in touch with it through meditation, leaning against the trunk or sitting nearby.

"Can I ask you what do you think about death?", I asked her after she had finished her explanation about Ogham. "I mean, are you scared about it?"

She often talked about that, but I couldn't understand what she felt.

"What a coincidence! One of my customers asked me the same question last week!", she exclaimed, starting making an herbal tea. She didn't drink tea anymore, just fennel, lemon balm or berries herbal teas.

"What do I think about death? Well, I'm damn scared about it. That's strange, as I consider it just a natural passage for our soul. We just change our point of view."
She went on. "In spite of that, the idea of leaving my body and getting to the other side of the veil really scares me. Besides the fact

that I'll have to leave my daughter, you and all my things here. I don't mean the things I own materially, but my habits. For example, when I'm dead I won't be able to talk like that anymore. I could maybe do it with the help of a medium. I don't want to discuss about that possibility, because I don't agree with it: we must let the dead find their peace, unless they decide to communicate with us, by dreams or somehow else."

"Do you know what happens to the soul after death?", I went on.

"From what I learnt in India and I read about pre-mortem experiences, the feeling is similar to the one of anaesthesia: our senses leave us, we can't feel anything on a physical level. We get into an exclusively mental dimension. Our soul is there, it can see without eyes and hear without ears. Dead people can clearly see their body from outside. That must be really overwhelming, but they aren't alone. Another soul approaches them in such difficult moments, to help them understand. It may be some dear person already dead or an angel, something like a messenger, a helper. The first days are very difficult both for the people who are left behind and for the dead ones, even if they don't have any idea of time. Everything is like a dream for them. They have to become accustomed with their new situation and leave the idea of their body. The dead takes part in his funeral. Moments of prayer and meditation are very important to help a soul get to the light. Many of them aren't ready to leave their life on Earth, there are many souls wandering because they can't find their peace. That's why cremation is so important, to make our separation from the physical aspect of Ourselves more solemn. Many religions consider a forty days' period as necessary for the soul to migrate to a new level of consciousness. There we'll be able to watch our past life as it was on a large screen, we'll analyse it and we'll be able to understand from a much higher point of view. Our dear dead's energy will never stop to support us and stay next to us from that new level."

"And then?", I knew Stella believed in reincarnation.

"It depends. If we need to, we can go back on the Earth."

"Why would we need to?", Sarah asked, after she had been keeping religiously silent all that time. She had been more serious for a few days, as if something was troubling her.

"Our soul needs different incarnations to learn, to get higher. If it didn't complete its journey towards Learning or didn't finish what it had come for, maybe in the case of a sudden death, so it can reincarnate. I like considering lives as a sort of school course. It gets more and more difficult while you go on. However, there are summer holidays between years. That's it, death for me is like a holiday when you can rest, regenerate and then start again."

"But why can't we remember our past lives?", Alison asked while she was spreading some butter on a slice of bread.

"That would be a real mess. How could you live a life well, when you're still thinking about the previous one? We can say that by regressive hypnosis, when we need it for our psychophysics well-being, we can get useful information about our past lives. The most difficult thing is being able to consider our life as a river flowing. We usually just consider the present, without considering ourselves as a part of a bigger plan."

My sister started crying at that moment, just like a river in flood.

"What the hell is happening to you?", I asked her.

"Have I said something wrong, Sarah?", Stella got up and handed some tissues to her. "Would you like an herbal tea? There might be still tea somewhere. I'm sorry, but I don't keep wine or any other alcoholic drinks at home."

"No, thanks Stella, I don't need anything. Its' just that...", she started sobbing once more. "It's just that you're all going away. I'm going to stay here alone. And talking about death made me feel very sad", she confessed downcast.

"We aren't going to die." I couldn't understand what was happening to her.

"No, you aren't. But you're going to London, Alison to Norway, Kiki is death and I'm staying here."

"Would you like to come with me during my gap year?", Alison asked with passion.

"No, thanks, I don't want to go anywhere. I'm ok right here and I don't understand why you all want to leave."

"Sarah, Reading is not the whole world." I certainly wasn't going to feel guilty because I was going to attend university twenty minutes far from home by train.

"Don't worry, I'll come back, I'll stay there just for a year", Alison whispered to her, sitting next to her and brushing her back.

"What if you prefer staying up there? If you find a Norwegian boy and don't come back anymore?"

"Then you'll come and visit me up there. But don't worry, I'm not going to spend all my life in Norway."

"Stella, would you like to read Tarots for me?"

"For her?", I thought. She should read them for us as we were leaving, not for her who was going to stay. I had really a mad desire in my heart to know how things would go on with Dylan, after I moved to London. But not just that: all about university, my friends, my accommodation. It was all so new for me. Even if I was really curious, I gave up because I loved surprises.

"Ok", Stella said going to fetch her cards. She lighted a stick of incense and a small candle. She might be trying to create an atmosphere or there might be a meaning behind her gestures.

She started mixing the cards and she asked Sarah to avoid crossing her legs. After my sister had lifted half of the cards, Stella took them and laid them down: she made a sort of cross, leaving some cards next to it in a row.

"Well, darling, you cards are talking by themselves. Look here: the "Tower" means the present, a change occurring in your life at the moment. Something steady which is going to break. Alison's and your sister's departure. There's also the "Hermit". You should learn to be by yourself. A change, a new job is coming soon", she said tapping her fingers on the "Wheel of Fortune". "Are you sending CVs? Are you doing anything?"

"I'm going to work for *Cath Kidston* as soon as I finish college."

That had been her goal for ages. " And to study drawing."

"Sarah can do wonderful fantasy drawings", I added.

"That's great. You could draw in your spare time, couldn't you?",

Stella warned her. "Your cards are really good. New possibilities are coming for you."

"And what about love?", she asked shyly.

"Nothing coming at the moment. You're young and beautiful. Love will come at the right time, don't be in a hurry."

"Are you a little less sad, now?"

"No, I'm not actually. The future scares me."

"That's usual at your age", Stella said in her motherly way. "Life is made of changes. You need them to grow up. Learning to go on without Alison and Anne will be very important for you. Come on, just remember you'll be able to hear them whenever you want."

She didn't need to be reminded. I was already expecting Sarah's hundreds phone calls at every moment of day and night.

XIV

The Cauldron

The end of college was coming very fast. We were going to be eighteen in May. We organized to go out with our friends on Saturday night and then we were going to have lunch at granny's house with our family. Luckily not all at the same weekend.

Following Alison's advice, we had dinner at a restaurant near the River Thames, where we could also dance. We were ten girls, all school mates.

As we had expected, people offered us some drinks, lots of drinks I should say, and we weren't used to drinking at all.

After a *Gin Tonic* and two *Mojito*, I stopped. I was having fun and I didn't want to overcome my limits. Sarah on the contrary let herself be dragged by the party. She started dancing barefooted on a table, then she went on throwing up on the shirt of a boy called Rupert, who unfortunately was crossing her way.

I heard him cursing, while she was squealing words like: "It's you who didn't let me go to the bathroom. You're really a naughty boy! And you're smelling vomit now! Naughty boy!"

"Stop drinking now, Sarah!", I warned her.

"Ok, everything is turning. Where's Rupert? He wasn't bad, was he?".

"You've just thrown up on him…"

"I have? Really? It's not possible." She was completely drunk. That made her nicer, luckily. She made us laugh till we cried. She started talking with a street lamp, then with the ducks. She kept saying nonsense. I had never seen her like that.

142

The next day we fully understood what having a hangover meant, especially my sister.

We spent the day on the sofa wearing pyjamas, eating sandwiches and drinking coke.

Dylan sent me a never ending series of messages. He even tried to call me, but I couldn't hear my mobile while I was at that party. He said he was studying, he was missing me and he was really looking forward to seeing me.

He was coming too for lunch at my granny's.

I hadn't seen him since September. I had been very busy with school that year and I hadn't gone to visit him anymore. I missed him, even if I heard him almost every day. It was difficult to consider as my boyfriend a boy I hardly ever saw. By the way, he was a part of myself and I was a part of himself. We got on well together, even if we were far away, because we knew we were there for each other. A very deep feeling was linking us and that was enough. Till then.

The cottage in May was a rejoicing of colourful flowers, busy bees, butterflies and delicious smells. We were born in a very beautiful month.

Granny had laid the table in the garden with violet tablecloths, colourful balloons and very nice paper decorations among the trees. She had really surpassed herself this time.

She welcomed us very brightly, hugging both of us. I could smell that delicious sweet lavender essence in her hair and the smell of apple pie, which brought me back to my childhood.

"My little girls have come of age." She hugged us once more, she was almost moved. I had never seen her cry, she was a real force of Nature. Nothing could upset her.

"Best wishes to my princesses. Here is my present: a box of strawberry candies", old Mal started saying.

"Oh Mal, thank you!", I told him.

"I did things in a big way for your eighteenth birthday."

Stella and Alison arrived soon after. They couldn't be missing, of course.

"Here you are, girls. It's a small present from my mum and me. She chose it", Alison told us, handing a packet to each of us. "They are the same, so you aren't going to quarrel", she went on.
It was a piece of amethyst. That was typical from Stella.
"Do you remember, girls? You can use it to purify home and put other stones on it, or something else, to charge them."
"Thanks, Stella", I told her with delight.
"Thanks." Sarah hugged her with gratitude. She was always more open-hearted than me.

We heard some footsteps on the gravel at that moment and Dylan arrived with two bunches of flowers. "Have I missed anything?"
My heart stopped beating. He was still more handsome than I could remember him. Eight months without seeing him had been very long. My legs were trembling.
"Come in, Dylan. It's presents time", his uncle welcomed him handing him a beer.
"So I've come at the right moment. Sarah, Anne, best wishes for your eighteenth birthday", he gave us the bunches of flowers. They were wonderful. There was a card on mine: *Best wishes, my princess. I've got another small present for you. I'll give you privately.* I blushed when I read it. I wondered what he had brought me.
He caught me by my shoulders at that moment and kissed softly my forehead.
"Are you ready to come to London?"
I was going to move in a very short time. I had decided to rent a room in a boarding house for students for the first years. If we kept getting on well, we could consider the possibility of living together then.

I had talked with him about it some months before and he had agreed with me, adding that he was going to come and visit me often in my rooms.

"I'm ready mentally", I told him. " But the organization is still unsatisfactory. I'm coming with my parents and visit the boarding house, I also need to understand where my university is. I'm going to live near Holborn and the university is the Westminster."

"Great, you can go on foot, if you wish. Are you going to stay at the Freemason's Hall by chance?", he asked me laughing.

"Where? I don't know that place."

"I'm joking. It's the general quarter of the most ancient Freemasonry in the world. A very beautiful and famous building. I'll take you there…"

I didn't understand what he was talking about, so I changed the subject.

"When are you going to graduate?"

"In a month. Then I'm going to start working as an accountant at *Liberty* shopping centre. Do you know it? Its offices are in Soho. We will be able to have lunch together or meet at the pub at night. It will be great, Anne, believe me! I could never leave London. Coming back home is very nice, leaving the big city for a while, the English countryside is wonderful, but I've told you again and again, London is magic and it's going to be still more with you."

"Come on! Lunch is ready!", my granny interrupted us, taking a hot baking pan of vegetable lasagne outside.

We spent a pleasant afternoon. One of the most beautiful birthdays I have ever had.

I was lucky I had such a close family.

"Ok, now it's time for our presents", mum claimed. "Come on Tom, let's give the girls our presents. Oh my God, eighteen years have passed from that hot afternoon in hospital…" The same old story every year. Mum always remembered how hot had been the day we were born.

"Here you are, from your father and me."

It was a single envelope. Sarah opened it, because she was besides herself with it. It might be a cheque or a flight ticket or…a ticket for Adele's concert at the O2 Arena…

"Wow! Thanks!", Sarah run to hug them. Adele? I wasn't crazy for her, but my sister was. So I took it easily and I thanked them with passion. They had always had the disposition to consider us as a single being: each of us should love the same things as the other. For instance pizza with cheese, which was my favourite but Sarah didn't like. In spite of that, mum always bought it.

"Do you like Adele?", Dylan asked me, when we were left alone in the living room for a while.

"No, well, she's a great singer, her voice is wonderful, but that's not my favourite kind of music. Sarah is very fond of her. My parents always think that we should have the same tastes, as we are twins." I smiled.

"Are you going to miss them?"

"Of course. It'll be the first time I'm far from home. I'm lucky you will be there", I told him very sincerely.

"Here you are, as I promised you." He handed me a small packet.

"Thanks, Dylan. You didn't need to…"

"Just open it. I hope you'll like it."

Oh, my God, it looked like a ring box. It couldn't be that. Was he going to make his proposal? Right there, at my granny's house? For my eighteenth birthday? I couldn't believe it!

He didn't go on his knees luckily and he didn't start telling words such as: "Anne, would you like…"

I opened it and I found a nice heart-shaped ring, hold by two hands with a crown above. I had already seen something like that. It was something Irish.

"It's very beautiful, thanks. What is it?"

"It's an Irish **Claddagh**. The hands stand for friendship, the heart for love and the crown for loyalty. I wish we could be these three things forever."

I thanked him, sealing my promise by a kiss. Being next to him was wonderful.

"You should put it on the ring finger on your right hand, as we aren't married yet.

Married? Did he say that world? Oh, my God! Was he talking about us?

"The point of the heart turning outside if you're a single, inside if you're engaged."

"Please, put it on my finger." I wanted him to celebrate that moment.

He slipped it on the ring finger in my right hand, the point turning inside. He kept staring at me, as if his soul wanted to be linked to mine. I felt excited every time our eyes crossed. That wasn't just physical attraction, there was something really much deeper.

"Anne", my granny was calling me.

"I'm coming", I answered in a trembling voice, without stopping looking at Dylan and at my ring. It really fitted very well.

We went out in the garden, where an almost blinding Sun and some clapping welcomed us.

It was cake time.

After an out-of-tune "Happy birthday to you", granny came closer with two gifts.

"This is for my little girls. Best wishes! I love you."

They were two small but heavy iron cauldrons, ten centimeters wide. They were really delicious.

"They're very nice, granny, thanks", I told her, kissing her cheek.

"Thanks. I'm moved", Sarah went on.

"Do you know why I have given you a **cauldron**? They're very nice pieces of furniture, of course, but they also have a deeper meaning."

We were all sitting and listening to her. Even Bell, which was very lively, was quiet on its own, under the oak, waiting to listen to its mistress.

"I've taught you everything my granny and my mum taught me, in these years. Just consider this small cauldron as a sign of my handing down my knowledge to you. You now hold all the things I know. In the cauldron in my kitchen, changes happen. I can make infusions, potions, "brews" as you call them, Anne. I can create and change. You've grown up and are changing. I hope you'll always use the tools I gave you. And since Stella has been very important for your education, I think it would be nice if you put the stone she gave you right into my cauldron.”

Sarah was crying and two big tears were going to fall from my cheeks as well. All the people there were deeply moved. Granny was always able to create a strong energy around herself.

“Thanks, granny”, were the only words we could say.

“I still have lots of things to teach you and I’ll certainly do it, all in due time. Let’s eat the cake now, or the cream will melt.”

“Let’s drink a toast for the twins!”, Mal exclaimed.

To be continued...

CONTENT

www.ingramcontent.com/pod-product-compliance
Lightning Source LLC
LaVergne TN
LVHW011015200726
843509LV00011B/1107